'...tive without resorting to caricature, the undercurrent
of violence never seems gratuitous, and the payoff is
perfectly-handled and nicely, darkly unsettling.'

JOANNE HARRIS, author of *Chocolat*

Daniel Shand was born in Kirkcaldy in 1989. He lives in Glasgow and works in Edinburgh, where he teaches at Napier University. His debut novel, *Fallow*, was published in 2016. It won the Betty Trask Prize and was shortlisted for the Saltire Society First Book of the Year.

www.daniel-shand.com

@danshand

Also by Daniel Shand

Fallow

CROCODILE

Daniel Shand

SANDSTONE PRESS

First published in Great Britain by
Sandstone Press Ltd
Dochcarty Road
Dingwall
Ross-shire
IV15 9UG
Scotland

www.sandstonepress.com

The publisher acknowledges subsidy from Creative Scotland
towards publication of this volume.

ISBN: 978-1-912240-37-1
ISBNe: 978-1-912240-38-8

Cover design by Stuart Brill
Typeset by Iolaire Typography Ltd, Newtonmore
Printed and bound by Totem, Poland

For Janey

PART ONE

HERE'S HOW IT GOES – HERE'S HOW SHE GOES. An engine ticks over in the street. The curtain's crack allows a sunbeam to show dust swirl over the living room, over crowded ashtrays, over mugs of thick and mouldy tea. Mum's palm grasps from the doorway, saying, come on, let's go.

The girl swings the rucksack over her shoulder and then she is through the door, out into the air, walking the fifteen steps – the fifteen trainer-smacks – along the path to the waiting car. All the while Mum's hand presses on her shoulder blade, urging, needling. The girl thinks goodbye to the bicycle rusting itself underground as she passes, goodbye to the exhausted birds' nests in the hedge's heart.

The woman in the passenger seat unlocks the back door and the girl slides in. She pulls the seatbelt across herself and thumbs the buckle into its housing. You can see her home's door standing ajar and there's this man in the driver seat – her grandfather. He revs the accelerator as the girl sorts herself and that sound's been coming for fifteen minutes now, all through getting ready. It hummed as she washed her hands in the spit-frosted sink, as she double and triple checked the contents of her bag. Come on, let's go, it said too.

Mum motions for the window to be rolled down, then pushes her face inside. 'Are you alright?' she asks, bunching balled fists into armpits. 'Comfy enough?'

The girl nods.

Mum nods too and directs her attention to the front. 'Listen,' she says. 'Thanks again. But really though.'

The girl's grandmother twists around and smiles. The loose skin of her neck contracts like a squeezebox. 'Oh,' she says. 'Settle down, Angie. You know we don't mind.'

The grandfather does not engage. He faces front.

'Aye,' says Mum, features narrowing. 'But I just wanted to say. And anyway, it won't be for long. Just for just now. Just until—'

'Aye,' nods her grandmother. 'Aye.'

Both women turn to the girl. This is where she's supposed to say goodbye, so she pulls herself up by the window frame and kisses Mum on the lips. Mum's eyes go reddish and she's pulling that face she pulls, her jaw working against its skin. 'Mind and be good for your granny and grandad.'

The girl recognises that same straining in her own jowls but breathes deep and holds it. Like counting the sound of her trainers, she knows this must be done. Everyone says their cheerios and the car pulls away. Mum waves for a moment in the rear-view mirror before hugging the cardigan tight around herself and scurrying up the path. The girl looks away when she notices the pair of bulbous pupils watching her from the mirror.

They drive on.

Here's her neighbourhood going past. Here's Raymond

Sinclair's house and the newsagents. Here's the post office and the flats where Fiona MacIntyre stays and here's the pet shop and the chippy and the tile factory where birds live and leave long streaks of white trailing from empty windows. Here's the wee park with the roundabout that you can get spun on till you're sick. Here's the bigger park where teenagers congregate and leave behind beer cans and aerosols.

Her grandmother shifts. Here it comes. 'Alright back there, pet?'

The girl nods.

Her grandmother turns to the right as she strains to witness the girl. Her grandfather's eyes look to her in the mirror again – ink spots dilated by the thickness of his glasses.

'How are you getting on at the school?' asks her grandmother, mouth open in anticipation of a reply.

The girl tells her fine. Her throat catches from not talking.

'Your mum sent us your report. Wasn't it good, Alec?'

'Aye,' says her grandfather. 'Good.' His voice is horrific, like blowing bubbles through milk.

'Ta,' she says. You can tell they want to ask about her mother, but they don't. Not for now anyway. Her grandmother maintains her sideways eye contact. 'Thanks,' the girl confirms.

'And it'll be the high school after summer, won't it?' says her grandmother.

'Uhuh,' says the girl.

Her grandmother's curls wriggle inside the headrest hole. The other contains the plasticky baldness of her grandfather's scalp, dappled with brown spots like drips from teabags. The hair's slick with oil.

Pressing the nail of her finger against the window, the

5

girl regulates the coldness she feels by the pressure she puts on the glass. She presses her fingernail against it, feels its coldness in the tip of the bone, in her cuticle. Touches her cheek against the glass. The camera she places out on the embankment catches her as the car zooms past. See the longing there. See the lonely fingernail. Perfect.

She plays a game to pass time. A red car overtakes, so another has to overtake by the time she counts to fifty or else their car will crash head first into something massive, immovable. The bonnet will rupture and the girl'll be encased in a cradle of biting steel, petrol spurting everywhere and ready to explode. She'll be pliered free by firemen but her grandparents will be absolute write-offs. Compound fractures, skulls crumpling – unless she sees red by fifty.

Panic sets in at forty.

Black. Black. White. Green. She's getting this picture of her organs – the liver, the pancreas, the stomach even – being squelched like fruit. She knows they're delicate these organs; it says so in her Body Book, the one she's too old for now. They're like these balloons of meat inside you and if she doesn't see a red car in five ... four ... three ... If she doesn't see a red car then her organs will be mashed alive in the collision.

A car, post-box coloured, comes from the opposite direction, which she counts. Which she has to count. It's cheating, but cheating's better than having your thigh bones crushed into fragments. Better than getting a bleed on the brain, like the telly sometimes shows. Sometimes Mum will be distracted or sleeping and she'll see these things on telly. For example: videos of surgery, or what happens if your body's DNA gets muddled and you're born all wrong.

'Oh,' says her grandmother. 'I never told you, did I Alec? About Her Upstairs?'

'Told me what?' he says.

'Did I tell you or not?'

'How do I know what you've told me if you don't say what it is?'

'You'll never guess what.'

He looks at the girl in the mirror. 'See what I put up with?' he says, addressing her for the first time.

'Her Upstairs has got herself a new one.'

'A new what?'

'A new man of course,' says her grandmother and the girl leans in to listen. 'She fairly gets through them, I must say.'

Her grandfather shakes his head in bafflement. 'How am I interested in that?'

'I just thought you'd want to know.' She looks to the girl, trying to draw her in. 'I'll just shut my face, will I?'

The girl allows a smile to show she knows they're not being serious. To show this is an old game: the gossiping wife and the irritated husband. She wishes they would carry on though, because she gets this restlessness from hearing about men and women and all the secret things they do.

And then through the window – somewhere she's been. She twists and gets close to the glass and her nose makes fog. It's that long stretch of water her mother took her to last summer, just after the girl hurt her foot. She was allowed to paddle and her mother drank wine and played music from the benches. A nice day, but then something nasty at the end. Something she can't now place.

The memory infuses her and she's thinking of tomorrow morning and how it'll be to wake up and not be able to go through into her living room and be alone and watch telly until her mother appears and they eat cereal together on the couch.

It's just as she's beginning to lose her mask that they turn into an estate where the buildings are all pale pink and yellow and her grandmother says, 'Here we are.'

She wants to ask something. She can't make herself say it.

But she's going to say it when the second hand on her watch hits the bottom, shows the *30*. She'll say it then – so she watches as the hand ticks towards her, so she counts under her breath. Here it comes. Now she'll say it, now she'll ask. And then the quivering hand points into her abdomen and her throat won't let the words up and already it's too late because the hand has carried on and it won't work if she speaks when it's showing the *40* or the *55*.

The car comes to a halt outside a house at the top of the street and as soon as the engine's off her grandfather gets out and is away up the path. From across the road three boys watch the car, one of them leaning on a pair of crutches. She looks away but can still feel their eyes on her.

She could just not get out. What would happen then? If she just refused to take off the seatbelt? I'm not going, she could say. It isn't happening. It could be done, couldn't it? They would have to take her back because – well – because they'd have to. It was the same as anything. How could they make you do something you didn't want to do?

Except they could do, couldn't they? In the end? It was like at the school when she hadn't wanted to get changed in front of the others one day. Look how that turned out. And anyway, she's already undoing the seatbelt and slipping from the car and carrying her rucksack. She's climbing the steps to the house, hearing this coming-and-going metalish whirr of a lawnmower or hedge trimmer somewhere off in the gardens. There's a similar, taller set of stairs to the right – the neighbour upstairs.

Inside smells like how her grandparents smell. How their car smells and how their bodies smell – a musk of soup and warm clothing. Their beaded curtain rattles on frosted glass as the door's closed behind her. Licks her lips and tastes the air. The dimensions of the hallway feel hazardous to her; heat creeps into her sinuses as she toes the plush brown carpet.

A hand on the neck. 'Well then,' says her grandmother and the girl turns to look. Wrinkles converge on her lips like rivers flowing to the sea. You can see this smiling coming through her eyes.

The girl nods.

'Let's get you settled in.'

In contrast to the warmth of the hallway, the room she's led into radiates coolness. Its walls are lined with chests made of gleaming woods and she puts her bag on the bed – the tight sheet springs.

'Here we go then. I hope it'll do you, pet. There's not much in the way of fun but anyway, it's just temporary, like your mum said.'

The girl opens a drawer in one of the units. The bottom is lined with wallpaper.

'Lots of room for dollies or whatever else,' says her grandmother.

The girl winces but nods. 'Aye.'

'I'll get the tea on,' says her grandmother, leaving the girl to settle in.

Placing her bag square in front of the bedside table makes her feel calm. She slips each trainer off with the toe of the other, still tied, and slides them beneath the bed. This calms her too. If she leaves things like this, she can be ready to go at a moment's notice.

Her mother had told her to listen. Asked her how she would feel about a nice wee holiday now that the school was off. Just until your mum's got herself sorted? Got her head together? Just until? And now this foreign room with nothing of hers. And now storage and tight sheets and whatever she managed to pack.

She lies down on the bed and closes her eyes. She sees her mother there, in the rear-view mirror, hustling up the path. When she's indoors, she says that the coast is clear and people come out from behind the couch and curtains and start to have a party.

This is great, says her mother, I feel so much better now she's gone.

All these adults, dancing and making drinks from alcohol and coming up to hug her mother.

The three of them eat their tea around a table built for two. The television laughs and applauds in the corner and the angle of its screen means the girl can see it reflected in all the framed photographs on the living room wall. She can see younger versions of her grandparents standing around a huge cake. She can see faces she doesn't recognise and a dog she's never met. There's one of her mother and a man and a baby.

'And so,' says her grandmother, dissecting a pad of meat. 'And so, I says to her, I says that's just typical, Barbara. That's just Barbara through and through, isn't it Alec?'

He nods without looking up from his plate. They're not used to making conversation like this. This is for her benefit. He looks beyond them both, glasses mirroring pulsing white light and the girl can make out the telly in them.

She tries to push this heavy meat and sauce into one corner of the plate because her stomach won't take it. At home the girl and her mother forage in the cupboards for whatever can be found: instant noodles, maybe toast for tea. There's butter or something in this sauce and it's coating her mouth and right into her belly.

Outside, the streetlights come on all together and her grandmother asks her to close the curtains. The three boys from before are still out there. They look up at the new streetlights, then nod to one another. Dispersing in separate directions, each boy's shadow stretches and releases as they pass beneath the orange lamps.

The girl can't tell if she's meant to sit and watch telly with them. She slouches on the couch and the plastic casing the furniture wears makes her T-shirt slip up her back. Closing her eyes halfway, she lets the room fade from focus. If she listens hard enough to the voice of the telly then she can stop hearing it at all and each syllable melds into the next. The camera she places out on the road zooms in past the curtains and catches her there, reclined in telly light. Perfect.

Maybe just now her mother is sitting on a bus or train, realising her mistake, coming to collect her. She's maybe pressing her own cheek against the glass and maybe the glass is splattered with droplets of rain. Come on, she'll say, throwing the door open, and they'll go back and stop in at the newsagent's and pick up frozen cheesecake and watch a film together into the night, like they sometimes do. She'll maybe even have cleaned up from the party and there won't be any men around forever.

It takes her some time to work up to the question. She counts down to it once or twice in her head, until, 'Is it alright if I just go to bed now?'

Her grandmother's attention snaps from the telly. 'Aye, of course it is, pet.'

She takes the girl through and shows her where the soap and toothpaste are kept in the bathroom. She gives her privacy so the girl can wash.

In lamplight and bound in blankets, she looks at one of the books she brought. She looks, but there's this feeling that something was left behind. She can't think what. She had to pack so quick that she might have forgotten something essential. Her mind crawls over its image of her bedroom at home, searching for lost items, until a creaking and the tread of footsteps comes from above … a murmur of conversation. She remembers what her grandmother said about Her Upstairs and the new man. Sounds die away. She closes her book and lets her eyes wander. After a couple of minutes, the ceiling begins to thud. This repeated *dum dum dum*. She knows enough to know what the sound means.

It becomes insistent, a nagging pounding that makes the girl feel so young and tiny and makes her want to bring the duvet up over her face. Though cloying and mouth-warm, she stays like that for a while, hearing the sound from upstairs, doing her best to ignore it. Having her head beneath the covers means she doesn't have to look up at that paleness and see the sounds coming through.

What she's keen to avoid, down there in the sheets, breathing in her own breath, is remembering similar sounds in the bedroom at home, where her mother's bedroom was right through the wall. At home, if her mother had visitors and those noises started to happen, she would do this floating trick. She would float and be someplace those noises couldn't reach.

When the humidity's too much she kicks off the duvet and the sounds stop and there's cool air on her forehead.

And then the room winks at her and she sees it happen.

It's alright, the room says.

What do you mean? asks the girl.

Them upstairs, they're not *at it* anymore.

The girl nods. Alright.

The room doesn't speak again and the people upstairs make no more noise and she manages to force herself into drowsiness – she holds onto the duvet with this tightness so that nothing exists but the holding.

The party's in full swing. The people in the crowd move around and have a fag, or whatever – the things they do at their parties – and her mother's the centre of the room. People push others out of the way for a chance to talk to her or hand her a drink and her mother relishes it all. She kisses everyone on their cheeks and tells these jokes and stories that drive everyone wild. What a laugh, they say, good her daughter's not here to spoil things for us. Her mother's sort of sitting on this guy's lap or something – maybe she's dancing – but then she spies something. Across the heads and faces of the party, beside the owl clock and the big candle, there's a photograph of the girl sitting by itself on the mantelpiece. In the photograph the girl's looking so lovely and pure that her mother's face falls.

She holds a hand across her chest and asks *What have I done?* and the girl turns over in her sleep.

SHE IS IN THERE, IN THE GRANDPARENTS' garden, near the boulders arranged ring-fashion round a bowl of plastic that looks like it was once a pond. Past that, a rectangle of neat grass and the shed. The girl steps up onto a largish boulder and jumps off, flailing her arms madly for the beat she's airborne. In the leap she sees over the fence to the grid of identical gardens that surround her – whirligigs and short trees and the roofs of sheds.

That first morning she made her breakfast in silence. Gripped her own thigh as she put margarine and marmalade on toast. The food was thick in her throat but she didn't know where to find a glass for water. In the hallway her grandfather was on his hands and knees, painting the skirting board. She could hear him breathe.

It was easy, it turned out, not to think about the noises from the night before. You could concentrate very, very hard on making the slice of toast look like the slice of toast on the margarine tub – like the perfect slice of toast. You could focus on that to make it easy to forget.

14

Likewise, if you used your whole brain to fall from the boulder and land in the dirt so that both your footprints were equally thick, equally defined ...

At home she would have been out with Raymond Sinclair and Fiona MacIntyre. They got up to all sorts. At home, you could get up to all sorts with, for example, a jam jar. Even stuff you felt was sort of babyish, like war. You could war bees, war wasps, war slugs. Even the green butterflies that flapped low over rhubarb could be warred.

Of all the beasties you could war it was obvious the best and most dangerous was wasps. A bee could sting but not with the same evil of a wasp. And a wasp could sting many stings compared to a bee's just one. It was harder to catch wasps. Something like a slug or a snail you could just scoop up into the jar. With wasps you'd have to sneak up to a bush with enough blisterings of pastel flower to attract them and you'd have to inch the jar around the flower so that the screwing on of the lid would behead it, trapping the insects inside.

You'd push that jar down onto the grass and you and Fiona and Raymond would gather round to see the things inside war. When they warred, bees and wasps would pump each other full of stings until they stopped and lay there, looking the same as when they were alive except not moving. You could war all the beasties you wanted until you look up at Fiona MacIntyre or Raymond Sinclair and see a leanness in their faces and you could begin to feel sort of scared by what was going on between you and you wouldn't be the first to suggest it, but if someone said warring stuff was rubbish and for wee bairns, you would agree and help to tip the black corpses from the jar.

From the boulder, she can see into the windows of the

upstairs flat. In the pane above the room she slept in, is the head and neck and shoulders of a young woman. Her hair is short and very dark and shines with a sort of shifting zebra-skin. The woman applies something to her lips, smoothes a palm down her hair. The girl can see she's wearing nothing but a bra on her torso. She watches as the woman stands and begins to button herself into a peach tunic from bottom to top, her narrow neck producing a second chin as she follows her fingers up her front until the top button is buttoned and she brings her face up and meets the girl's eye.

The girl winces, looks away, pretends to study one of the boulders, waits for the next movement to come to her. Waits for the next movement to come. They meet each other's eye again. The woman sticks her tongue out and the girl can see she has a piercing there.

In a stranger's garden, the day fills with wet heat. Afternoon sky mutates from pressure as areas of cloud swell and discolour, as gaps form further off and let smears of light through. It's like a raised hand to the girl's back and causes sweat to bead there. She has to lean so that the swing she's standing on won't tip her off. It's just a wee bairns' thing and the seat's shaped like a crocodile head, but from her position she can see into the next garden over.

'Naw naw naw,' goes the one in crutches, bending and pointing at the ground between the three boys. 'You're messing it up, Chris. The nail goes in at that end or else you've got nothing to pull the band on.'

The boy on his knees, Chris, lets the hammer drop. 'Who's doing it?'

'Eh?' responds the boy in crutches.

The third boy looms over the other two, amused or confused by their bickering.

'Who's doing it? You or me?' says Chris.

The boy with crutches takes a step back. 'What're you trying to say?'

'I'm saying, Ally, if you want me to do it then shut up and let me do it.'

Ally interrupts him with a wave of the crutch. 'Oh, fine then. I'll just sit here and keep quiet when I notice my mate fuck up a project before my very eyes. That makes total sense.'

'Maybe you want to do it yourself?' says Chris.

'Obviously I don't want to do it myself,' says Ally, brandishing a crutch. 'Don't start blaming me for my conditions.'

Chris screws up his face. 'Aw, don't give me that.'

'Give you what?'

'Give me hassle about your you-know-what.'

'So just get on with it.'

'So just shut your face,' says Chris, raising the hammer.

Ally closes his eyes. 'Fucksakes. All this hassle for a fucken nail gun. Would you just get on with it please?'

He gets beside the third boy and they watch as Chris hammers home the nail. The boy Ally never stops moving, not for a second. Adjusting and readjusting his weight on the supports and sort of scowling and moving around the boy on the ground and there's something about him. This furtive pale head and a paunch to his lips and eyelids, the segments of his gnarled arms moving.

The tall boy – she hasn't made out his name – smiles as Chris rises from the ground and presents the *thing*. The nail gun.

'Give it to me,' goes Ally, transferring both crutches to

an armpit and grabbing it from the boy Chris. 'Who's got something to shoot?'

Chris pulls a stone from his pocket. He lets Ally grab it and fiddle with the nail gun while holding both crutches and the girl stands on tiptoe on the swing's seat. She pulls herself up by the chains, feeling without seeing that the clouds are piling up and extinguishing all glows of the world above. This faint chill of wind touches her knuckle.

'There it is,' goes Ally and he brings up the gun – this stubby plank of wood with some nails hammered into the sides and top. All boys follow the direction that Ally points and, in the second before a twang rings out across the gardens, the girl makes eye contact with each of them in turn.

She falls backwards from the swing and hits the grass and opens her eyes and sees the crocodile swing back and forth from the force of her fall. The feeling is more a panic than any kind of sharp, physical pain. The swing swings back and forth, creaking like laughter, and Chris appears above the fence, along with the fingers he's used to hoist himself up.

She can hear the other one, Ally, going, 'Who the fuck was that?'

Chris eyes the girl, his chin resting on the wood. 'It's a lassie.'

A soft gust brings something cold to life on top of her head. She can hear her breath now as she brings her fingers up to touch the coldness. No blood yet, but this wicked sting's starting to throb from her crown.

Chris looks behind himself. 'I think she's hurt.'

'She's hurt?' goes Ally's voice. 'Well, that's hardly my fault, is it? How am I meant to know she's standing in the way of the gun?'

'I think that's shocking,' goes a deeper voice – the tall one. 'That makes you a lassie-basher, Ally.'

The gentle tickle of running fluid above her eyeline. The swing swings back and forth and the boy Chris … his face framed by these bars. She stands and pats at her parting. Warm and wet and when she brings her fingers down she sees they're coated in redness with one yellow hair clinging to the mess.

Higher, shriller, Ally's voice saying, 'That fucken gun hurt me as well, you know. Tell her, Chris. I think it chipped me on the fingernail.'

Chris isn't listening. 'Fuck, she's bleeding,' he says. 'Are you alright?'

Up from her throat comes the sob she's been holding in since the crack of elastic on nail and wood, since falling backwards with closed eyes, since the shockwave of impact juddering down her jaw.

'You bastards,' she says, turning, and as she darts down the path by the neighbour's house, she hears Ally going, 'What's happened? Is she away? Is she going to tell on us, Chris?'

The girl's face burns with shame. Fury at letting them see her tears. Her eyes and the top of her head made cold again by their moistness as air moves over her running body.

Her grandad pats down the hair on either side of her head, trying to calm her and reveal the injury there. 'Shush,' he says.

'Sorry,' she says.

He holds her head so she's looking him in the eye, confused by her apology. 'There's no need to tell me you're sorry, hen. I was only saying.'

What she wants to say, what she can't say, but what she's saying over and over inside is: *I want my mum*. It's repeating in there, rattling about in her mind since the stone bounced off her skull.

She's remembering the fingers of her mother's hand dancing across the face of their remote control, selecting channels and moving a fag away from her lips. She's the most beautiful woman the girl knows – all the boys go quiet when she collects the girl from school, on the days she shows up. She's remembering curtains closed against whatever might harm them and small lamps sending discordant shadows out from all the knick-knacks: the porcelain fairy on the fireplace, the chain of rubber dolphins, CDs piled a metre high. This was what home meant. It meant safeness and that mother-heat. Mum's face turning to the girl and all light in the room going dim and only her mother's face being illuminated and speaking with her voice of how cigarettes smelled.

Her grandad continues to dab at the injury with a flannel and the wet trickles down. 'That better?' he asks, wringing the cloth into a basin, water the colour of pink socks.

She nods.

'Brave lassie.' He stands, supporting his back with one hand. 'Wanting some juice?'

'Aye. Please.'

He carries the basin out and she perches on the edge of the couch. *I want my mum*. She says it out loud in the quietest voice, only barely sound and the air of it tickling her lips with its delicacy. He comes back and she drinks the juice.

'How do you get a crack on top of your head by an accident?' he asks.

She wipes her mouth with the back of her hand. 'I wanted to see how high I could get the stone.'

She could tell him the truth, and then what would happen? He'd march across the road to tell off the boys? Or else maybe make her feel she's making a fuss over nothing, make her feel she's too soft and shouldn't even bother leaving the house if she can't cope with the world beyond?

'Huh,' he says. 'Bairns.'

The last time she'd been hurt was at the school. None of her friends from home went to her school. Fiona MacIntyre and Raymond Sinclair went to ones further away because of their families' religions or money, so it was lonely at break and you couldn't be daft and war bees or play soldiers like at nights.

There wasn't any reason to have climbed the tree, was the thing. It wasn't as if Abbie McMurdo or Lesley Philips were chasing her about, wanting to ask her in front of people if she knew what a blowjob was and then laugh at her whatever the answer was. It was like she started to climb the tree because she wanted to be the type of girl who'd just climb a tree if the fancy took her, because she saw the world in a different way to the rest of them, the other bairns that saw the world through clouded glass.

It was easy to climb, narrow and rangy as she was, hoisting herself from bough to bough, feeling the green tree-dirt stick to her palms and not even caring. Below her was probably a gaggle of students gazing up, not clapping yet but giving off the energy of a group who could be tipped into applause at any second. She didn't look down, savoured instead the anticipation of turning and seeing them all from the very top.

She's remarkable, someone would say.

Have you ever seen such an authentic display of physical prowess?

That's the kind of lassie I'm inviting to my next birthday party.

She would reach the top of the tree and everyone on the ground would be calling up to her, shouting her name, and she'd be waving down and laughing. You would see Abbie McMurdo and Lesley Philips, up at their bit by steps, watching her with fury. How dare she be grown-up enough to climb the tree? How dare she show them up like that? Nearing the top, she was so excited. Her fingers were trembling from how good it would be to see their anger.

But then: dread deep as the bell rang out, saying it was the end of break. She looked out across the grass to see dispersing groups of students and no one at all beneath the tree. She squealed under her breath and lobbed herself downwards, hands and soles connecting with the correct branches and eyes moving between hands and the emptying playground and performing small drops to reach the necessary branches. She swore as she reached the tree's lowest portion and saw the drop below.

A blankness of thought.

Not thinking that a reroute around the tree for a safer drop would make her what, a few minutes late? Not thinking of the solid dirt beneath her or that the teacher wouldn't care if she missed the first five minutes. Not thinking of anything at all, she crawled from the branch and let herself hang. Landed to instant pain, felt a crunch in her foot as she fell on it sideways. Some others saw her fall and ran inside to get someone and a teacher came out and they crowded round and asked her what had happened.

22

She had nothing to say.

The nurse fitted her with a cast and bandages and that same night she moved into the light of her mother in their living room, feeling the warmth and smell of her. Mum blew breath across the ankle to let her powers speed the healing process and it worked. Her mother's sweetness entered her pores and worked its way down to the bone and reconnected the torn parts. There were no words for how that felt. It was this damp heat and it curled around her ligaments and tendons and nursed them whole.

Sounds painful, goes the bedroom.

The girl opens her eyes from remembering. Aye, she says, it was.

The room coughs. And what did she say?

She tightens her grip on her hands. She wasn't happy, she says.

The room laughs. I bet. And how did you get that gash on your bonce?

She tells the room what happened and it winces. They're just a pack of bastards, she says.

Maybe, it says, or maybe it was a mistake.

Well, she says. It doesn't even matter. I'll be away soon – what do I need them for? She's coming now, she's always coming.

DESPITE THE PAIN IN HER HEAD, she keeps an eye out for the boys. She perches on the couch and occasionally glances through the window, hoping she'll spy them lurking under the streetlight again. There's little else to do here. Her grandfather went into the shed after breakfast and her grandmother's working through the paper's puzzles. At home she'd have been out already, wandering the pavement, looking for friends. Her mother often sleeps in and sometimes the electricity will have finished, meaning there's no point staying indoors.

Her grandmother folds over the paper. 'You bored, pet?'

'No.'

'You are bored,' she smiles. 'Let's go out.'

Inside the supermarket is the same as the one at home. Same light, same trolleys, same faces of adults looking at everything at once. Her grandmother shops methodically, travelling an aisle at a time, scanning the shelves for deals. The other shoppers must think it's strange that the girl's here with her grandmother in the holidays. Why's she not out with pals? Hasn't she got any? Is she a bit . . . you know?

She's worried hard about rounding a corner and seeing Abbie McMurdo say or Lesley Philips, standing there together in maybe the toiletries aisle, comparing all the shampoos with their heads of very straight, very shiny hair together in discussion, until they look up to see the girl standing there. It doesn't matter that she's however many miles from home – it's a possibility. They'll look up and their noses will screw and they'll say, Look at the state of her. Has she not heard of a washing machine or hair-straighteners?

'Is it alright if I look at the magazines?' she asks.

'Course you can,' says her grandmother.

She cuts through an empty checkout to get to the magazine bit. There's a few bored-looking men loitering by the magazines – such blue jeans, so many lumps hanging over the backs of belts. The girl moves between them, picks up a magazine and opens it halfway through. After flicking through a few pages, she sighs. It's all bairns' stuff.

She loves magazines – absolutely adores them. You can show up at the wee post office and depending on the day you know the ones they'll have. A pathway lined with overhanging trees – Jimmy's Loan – connects her street at home to the street with the post office. Mum makes her promise not to use it as a shortcut because of its bad feeling, because of the leaf litter and used johnny wrappers. She sneaks up there anyway and gets these knives of guilt in her stomach from it. Sometimes, if she's lucky, her mother'll give her money for four, five issues. Other times she'll look at her with black bags under her eyes and go, 'A magazine? Is it not enough to feed and clothe you, like?'

That's not a nice thing to think of, so she puts the magazine back. Around her, the sound of talking and of trolleys shunting and of price guns and of the in-store radio telling the girl how much oven chips are in the freezer aisle. She notices this one called *MIZZ 16*. The girl on the cover looks healthy and wholesome and also like she doesn't care about looking healthy and wholesome. Casts an eye around to see who's watching, takes the magazine from the rack. *MIZZ 16* promises she'll be able to find out if *He Really Likes Her*, what the top ten songs of the summer are. Air blows about inside her with the excitement of it. Closing the magazine, she sees these things:

> her mother's profile, in a cloud of telly-lit fag smoke
> the woman upstairs in the window
> a face and fingertips appearing over the top of a
>   garden fence.

So she moves along the centre of the supermarket, its bustling spine, looking left and right down each aisle for her grandmother. When she sees her, she'll go right up to her and show her *MIZZ 16* and say, Is it alright if I get this? It only costs ... however much it costs.

When she finds her, Gran's down at the bread. The girl pauses at the end of that aisle, watching her compare two loaves. She's going to go up and ask her when she counts to ten in her head. Not a second before or after – going up to her at say nine or eleven could throw the whole thing off.

She counts then, leaving gaps between the numbers, but at ten she doesn't move. By now her grandmother has dismissed both breads and has picked up a third.

That first ten was a practice though. Again, faster

now, letting each number run into the next. Grips the magazine, looks around the pile of tins. Again. *Onetwothreefourfivesixseveneightnineten.*

Again, faster, squinting.

Inside, she sees herself asking. She tries to cloud out her own begging face of wanting with endless chanted numbers. The counting's like a water you can drown badness in, this sort of pushing noise wave, and she tries to float up the shame of asking, but it's too heavy. It sinks down and fills her vision and she can't let it happen. She turns and moves down the supermarket's backbone and the same cold dread is filling up her insides as when she climbed the tree. This pelvic giddiness coming from her inability to tell what's coming next.

Of course though – she's seen her mother do it. She's never made a big deal of it, but the girl's noticed. Noticed the use of her mother's finger to inject a tube of mascara up into her sleeve. Noticed the removal of a price tag from the top her mother's wearing, standing seven shops down from the Topshop they've just left. Noticed the cheesecake hidden within a cereal box as she helped Mum unpack.

She lets her own feet and trainers make the choices for her and turns down the first empty aisle she meets. It feels slippery in the crook of her elbow now, the magazine. Feels liable to fall from her grip and make a slap on the tiles as heads turn and open their mouths. She unzips her jacket as she walks, stops in front of the DIY bit, and eyes the hammers and the tape measures. She swallows and blinks. Batteries are three for the price of two. Her abdomen pulses and she slips the magazine inside her jacket and zips it in. She can feel it curve around her ribs and the top of her hip and she takes a set of pliers down and reads the label. Heavy and cool on her side, the magazine holds her loins like a palm, stuck to her by the jacket's pressure.

She bites the inside of her cheek.

Her grandmother's at the freezers, fishing a box of lemon ices from the bottom. 'Hello pet,' she says as she stands, her glasses foggy with cold. 'See anything?'

'No.'

'Well, that's me finished anyway.'

The girl helps to push the trolley down to the checkouts and as they turn at the aisle's end her grandmother pulls them towards one specific till.

'Hello Karen,' she says to the woman there – the neighbour upstairs!

'Alright Margaret?' goes Karen, looking up from the paper she's writing on. Her face is open and skin clear. She palms her hair. 'How're you getting on?'

'Fine, fine,' says the girl's grandmother, as she begins to load the shopping onto the belt. 'And yourself?'

'Can't complain,' she shrugs and begins to scan the shopping.

The girl helps to unpack the trolley. She feels a sharp tug on the rug beneath her, like it's about to be pulled. What if, as the girl leans across, a gap opens up beneath her jacket and the magazine sprawls out, sending pages flying?

'Just doing away,' continues Karen. 'Working. They've got me on this awful shift pattern.'

Her grandmother shakes her head. 'That's terrible. But were you not up at the college before?'

What if, also, Karen leans into the girl's grandmother and taps herself on the nose and says something like, You'll never guess who was spying on me the other morning?

'Aye, well, no. I was. Not anymore.'

'You didn't like it?'

28

'It was all the politics that comes with it. When you were doing the actual subject, I loved that. But it was all the added-on stuff I couldn't stick.' She catches the girl's look and opens her eyes to her and cocks her head. 'So this is the lodger?'

The girl tries to smile because she can tell she's being teased.

'That's right,' says her grandmother. 'Our wee grand-daughter, Chloe. Though not so wee anymore. Her mum's not too well just now, poor thing.'

The girl's ears prick up at this. At any mention of her mother. She transfers milk up onto the checkout, feels the magazine against her bones.

'Nothing serious?' asks Karen.

'Oh no. Nothing like that.'

In her quickness to answer the girl can see she's ashamed. Doesn't even know what it is that's wrong, there's no name for it in the Body Book, but can tell what it means by how her grandmother talks.

Karen gets up from her stool and reaches across the till. 'A pleasure to meet you.'

The girl laughs at the formality and shakes the hand, feeling the skin of it to be very smooth and delicate and feels her own glide away from its gentle grip.

'Listen,' Karen's saying. 'If you're ever bored or fed up you can come up to mine for a bit. If your gran and grandad say it's alright?'

The magazine's corners work at her skin and she's shivering and nodding and feeling its angles press against her own.

Breath floods out of her as she closes the bedroom door, breath tainted by vacuum-sealed chicken breasts and fluorescent lighting. Crosses the room in six paces. Expects and accommodates the creak on the fourth – closes the curtains. Their pattern is made washed out and sort of sad-seeming by the brightness showing through. When she feels the magazine pressed to her side, she sees her mother reach behind herself to tear the price tag from her top.

In the dark, she lays the magazine down on the bed, strokes its face. The magazine has a folded corner that she bends back and remembers...

She lies down on her bed at home, in her own room, and her mother strokes her face. She tucks her into bed with a kiss on the forehead. 'I'm going out tonight,' she's saying. 'Don't answer the phone – it's an adventure.' She's holding her finger to her lips as she closes the bedroom door and then it's blackness. The girl's excited for a while, imagining what secret journey her mother's on. She's maybe out in the woods and poaching pheasants like in that book – maybe she's only running to the shop for a few messages but she wants to make it fun for the girl.

She gets bored waiting and goes into the living room, then the kitchen and her mother's bedroom. Everything's empty. There are no lights. She stifles a cough and climbs into bed – she's going to show her mother how big she is. They're two girls together and they speak the same language. So what if one of them slips out into the night? Her mother's going to find her sleeping and be so proud.

In her grandparents' house, she lifts up the mattress and slides the magazine above the bedframe. She can feel her rabbity heart beat in the structures of her neck. Another time, she found this bird out on the front step, left by

30

cats. It had a wing gone and was bleeding from puncture wounds. She picked it up without thinking, a songbird as light as polystyrene, and her thumb brushed its soft, smoke-coloured breast and you could feel its heartbeat going like nothing else. So quick and powerful and there was just so much there.

And as its heartbeat slowed, so too does hers.

It was a mistake to have left the magazine beneath her mattress. All night long she surfed between sleeping and not, feeling it there like a cold slab in the space below her. Can't even risk reading it when she's awake, just in case her grandmother bursts in and finds her hunched over like a pervert, reading slack-jawed about boys in a seam of milky dawn.

Instead, the girl lies on her side, a thick collar of duvet at her throat and senses it beneath her. She eats breakfast alone, and then showers. Puts her hair in a pleat still wet.

To four, and then she'll say it. To four and then she'll say. One. Two. Three. Four: 'What was Mum like?'

Her grandfather peers at her through the shed's solid air and coughs liquid. 'Eh?'

Hair damp and with her socks slipping down inside her trainers, the girl looks down the garden path behind her, then back to the shed. Larger and darker in there than she'd imagined and her grandfather in his shirtsleeves and braces on hands and knees.

'It doesn't matter,' she says.

He sits back on his heels and transfers mucus to his handkerchief with much audible effort. 'Hold on,' he coughs. 'What was it?'

'I was wondering if you could remember? What Mum was like, when she was wee?'

He laughs and shakes his head and turns over the lawnmower he's been working on, right side up. The pupils beneath his glasses are black eggs and the sawdust in the shed's air collects in the wrinkles of his face, these healed cuts from age.

Her mind shows her something then, something she ties together with this fear going through her. She's in bed at home and low voices and music are coming through the door to the living room. The room is underwater with darkness, complete but for the lines of light present at three sides of her door. It's these she looks at as she listens, rigid and pale in the inky aquarium of this memory.

'I don't like talking about it,' says her mother.

The reply is less distinct, deeper and more easily consumed by the fuzz of music.

'It was a bad time,' her mother says, calling the other by their name, which the girl can't remember. 'It was bad for me.'

A response. The girl turns over and onto her flank. Quiet about it, at the risk of breaking the spell of whatever's going on outside. She has her hands flat together between her thighs and she shivers.

'Aye. I am still angry about it. Don't give me any of your hippy forgiveness shite.'

More deep voice.

33

'Aye, well that's easy for you to say with your—'

...

'I am calm.'

...

'Listen: he used to hit me. All of the fucken time. My dad did. I still have scars.'

...

'You don't know how it was for me back then. You don't know how scared I was.'

And then the girl's back peering into the shed and the old man in front of her looks harmless, incapable of quick temper or violence; he's near mute, doddering. She remembers his silence in the car though. There had been a sharpness to it, hadn't there?

'Was she naughty?' the girl asks.

Chuckling like pebbles in riverwater. 'Aye. You might say that,' he goes, cleaning his gnarled fingers on a rag. 'See. She always used to go about with this one. They were – what is it they say? – thick as thieves? Whenever your granny got called up the school, it was for the pair of them. They were always bunking off and doing God knows what. Must have been two, three years older than you at the worst of it. Anyway, one night I come in after work and she's – your mum's – sat at the kitchen table and her hands and face are all red.'

He shows the girl his palms and runs a finger over his cheek.

'And your gran's off the wall with it. Alec, she's saying. Alec, what are we gonnae do, see? Like that. So I says to her – to your mum – I say, what's happened? What've you been up to now? She won't say. Always quiet. So I ask her again, and she still won't say. Then your gran tells me what's happened – that your mum and her pal've

34

tried to shoplift John Dick's shop and he's sprayed them all with paint.'

The girl opens her eyes and he nods.

'What happened?' she asks.

'She's been bunking off with the other one and they wanted a pack of fags or whatever and they've went in John Dick's with tights on their heads like *gangsters* and pretending they've got knives and John Dick's sprayed them down when he's seen what's up. They've gone running, hidden out in this field all day trying to get the paint off or something.'

'Wow.' The word slips out.

'You wouldn't be wowing if you had John Dick calling round.'

She asks him what he did with her mother and he fiddles with the glasses again. 'I lost my temper,' he says and he looks past her and touches the baldness of his crown.

He used to hit me, all the time, says her mother through a bedroom door, through a memory.

He turns from her, wipes his hands on the front of himself. Very veined, very pink. All around his head are pots of paint stained the colour of their contents.

She lets herself fall backwards onto the grass and lies there with her legs out in front and hands behind and faces the sky so that her closed eyelids show red and she can see all of the delicate and queasy connections of capillaries within. She concentrates so hard that she can see her own heart's beat in the backlit strands of vein. A wind blows through her inner ear, through the labyrinth of whorls and hammers.

Carry on like that and you'll go blind, says her mother's voice, ringing and whirling in her head, in her eyes.

35

Sorry, the girl says, but she doesn't move.

Fine, goes her mother. Wait and see. Her voice sounds distorted, like she's talking through a mouthful of water. How're you getting on?

The girl says, Fine. You'll be having a blast without me, I suppose?

Aye. I am. It's better not having you here.

I thought so, says the girl and she moves her head around on its neck and the purpling and exploding lights move with it and she needs to open her eyes. I suppose you're hoping he's going to batter me as well?

I just want to shag my boyfriends and I don't mind if you end up getting hit.

The girl's lids fight against her, battling in small, consistent ways to get her to burst them open and let in the sky. She's sitting so still and the creatures in her kneecaps and her elbows and hips tell her to use them, to bend and enjoy them. She doesn't listen. Just locks her joints and listens.

I want you away for as long as possible, her mother says, and the embers in her joints burn and the insects in her eyelids pull back and reveal fingernails of muffled sunlight, all lash-blurred and messy.

What's *wrong* with you? asks the girl.

What's wrong with you? her mother asks back.

The more the girl has to concentrate on the not-opening of her eyes and the not-moving of her body the more her mother's voice falters.

What's wrong with you? *Wh*-what's wrong to you? If – if – wrong with you?

And then the girl doesn't fight it anymore and her eyes are opened and she is dazzled by sunlight and she collapses on her back and jiggles her limbs around.

36

When she sits back up, there they are – the three boys.

'She's spazzing out,' says Chris.

'That stone's knackered her,' says the tall one.

Ally just scowls. 'Alright grass?' he asks and the girl goes from glancing at each one in turn to gazing at the ground.

What she wants is something to say but her brain stalls and stutters and she goes, 'I didn't grass,' in a voice like tissue.

Ally scoffs. 'Aye, I'm sure. That's exactly what a grass would say in this scenario, grass.'

The boy Chris rubs at his jaw. His skin is darkish. 'Ally.'

Ally waves a crutch at him. 'Naw don't, mate. A grass is a grass is a grass. They'll say anything to save their own skin. Believe me – I've dealt with my fair share of grasses in my time.'

'I didn't,' goes the girl.

'How can we be sure?' demands Ally, hen-like in his fluster.

She shrugs.

'Your cut alright?' asks Chris.

She touches the wound without meaning to, then nods.

'Sorry about that,' he says.

'Are you soft in the head?' goes Ally. 'What're you saying sorry for? She's the one that grassed us up!'

Back out on the street at home with Raymond or Fiona there was the comfort of being with people you'd known since before you could remember and you knew the gardens like the back of your hand. You knew who was a friend and who was an enemy and even if Raymond and Fiona would sometimes bicker among themselves, you were good

37

at stepping back from them, stepping up into the platform of your mind where you could watch them fight and the sounds coming from their mouths would be noise.

Ally pokes a crutch into her shin. 'Eh? How can we be sure you're trustworthy?'

She thinks back to the shed. To the prickle of fear she'd felt there. 'If I'd grassed you'd know all about it. My grandad's mental.'

'How's that?' asks Chris.

'He used to be a boxer,' says the girl, the lie speaking itself from her mouth.

This has an immediate effect on Ally, who stops his shuffling motions as soon as she says it. 'Did he? The old boy? He's – was – a boxer?'

The girl nods.

'My dad was a boxer,' goes Ally and Chris tuts at him, saying, 'No way.'

Ally nods, defiant. 'He's got one of them cauliflower ears.'

'Getting your head kicked in all the time doesn't make you a boxer,' says Chris.

'Pish, he was. He got run out of the game since he wouldn't throw a fight. All these mobsters were saying he had to fall in the third but my dad's not like that. He stuck to his guns and had to pack it in.'

The tall one, ignoring the argument, gears up to say something, pupils moving between Ally and Chris and the girl on the grass. His eyelids are shiny and his lashes strangely luscious.

'There's this treehouse up the woods, apparently. We're going for a look,' he says to the girl. 'You should come.'

Ally quits his quarrel with Chris and rounds on the tall one. 'What are you playing at, Darryl?'

'Eh?' goes Darryl.

'What are you playing at letting a grass know about the treehouse?'

Darryl blinks. He smacks his lips.

The girl counts to five, then says, 'Can I see it?'

Over his shoulder, vertebrae visible in the skin between collar and curls of hair, Ally goes, 'One hundred per cent not. I'll be dead in the ground before I show a grass where our treehouse is – before I've even seen it myself!'

'She could just come and have a look, man,' says Chris.

'Oh, I get it!' says Ally. 'It's like that is it? Ganging up on Ally cause his legs don't work proper? This one giving away the gang's secrets and this one agreeing with him.'

'Christ, man,' goes Chris. 'We're only saying it's hardly the end of the world if she comes just for a look.'

'I see how it is,' says Ally, shaking his head, eyes skyward, shifting himself backwards away from the rest. 'Well let's do it then. C'mon grass, let's go. Let's just go, and don't you two dare blame me once the secret's out and we've got every arsehole from St Christopher's or Homemuir hanging about at our fucken treehouse.'

They exit the estate and wait at the dual carriageway separating them from the woods on the other side. Chris holds up his arm and she can tell what'll be expected of her – to run out into the road when a gap appears. There's nothing she can do about it and she does her best to banish her grandmother's face.

Roars and moans come from the cars as they barrel by, the space they leave behind filled with smoke and snatches of the radio.

'Now,' shouts Chris and they all run out into traffic and the girl blanks her mind.

Lining the path through the woods are all these mushrooms – little clusters of brown ones in the grass and great white shelves of them jutting from tree trunks, undersides black and combed. The boys don't notice as they charge through the undergrowth, but the girl sees them and their multitude and feels threatened. The trees on either side are close and the sky appears above them as a pale, ragged strip. Muffled sounds of movement from the canopy cause the girl to imagine the leaping and landings of squirrels or birds perched high up, unsteady and fat on branches.

Ally's still in a huff. He keeps trailing behind and pretending not to be able to get over logs, then he'll get angry when Chris and Darryl offer to help. 'Thanks a lot,' you hear him shout, struggling with some new obstacle. 'Thanks a lot for leaving me here to nearly break my leg getting over this fucken mess. I suppose it'd be better for all you lot if I just died, wouldn't it? That'd be pretty ideal for you.'

'Is he alright?' the girl asks.

'He's fine,' says Chris, moving a branch to let her and Darryl pass. She's noticed Darryl's bottom lip is scaled and sunburnt-looking from his habit of running his tongue over it when concentrating.

'Maybe I should just go back,' shouts Ally. 'Since no one's wanting to wait on me?'

'He'll get over it once he sees we're not stopping,' adds Chris.

Eventually though, they have to stop and look back and you can see that he's not managing this one huge trunk in the path. He's dropped a crutch and it's out of his reach on the far side of the fallen tree.

'Come on, mate,' goes Chris and he helps Ally over.

'I'll have those,' he says, taking the crutches, and then, to Darryl, 'Right big man.'

Baffled, Ally watches as Darryl gets down on one knee, facing away from him.

'I'm not getting on his dirty back, if that's what you're suggesting,' says Ally.

Darryl looks over his shoulder. 'Come on,' he says.

Ally stares at Darryl, his mouth an outraged twist.

'It's not gay, if that's what you're thinking,' says Darryl.

'It isn't gay,' agrees Chris, tucking the crutches into his armpit.

'I'm not saying it's gay,' goes Ally. 'I don't care if it's gay. I'm telling you that I'm not going on his back. Not now, not ever.'

Further down the path, Chris leans in to her. 'How long've you been at your gran and grandad's for?'

The girl moves to one side to let Darryl and Ally lumber ahead of her, the wee chap gripped to the tall one's back.

'Oh, not long,' she says.

'And how come you're staying down here?'

Ducking beneath a branch lets her avoid his eye. 'My mum gets so busy with work that I have to sometimes. She doesn't like it but it's an important job she's got.'

'Right,' says Chris.

'In all these businesses,' she adds.

'It was Darryl's big brother told us about this place,' says Chris. 'This is where they all used to come to hang out when they were younger. It's supposed to be quality.'

'We had this treehouse back home,' says the girl.

'Oh aye?' says Chris. 'What was it like?'

'Just like how you'd expect,' says the girl.

'Oh,' says Chris. 'Right.'

What can she say? Can hardly bring up Raymond and

Fiona and warring bees on the grass like bairns, can she?

From his elevated position on Darryl's back, Ally starts to shout. 'There it is,' he says. 'Fuck! There it is.'

Ahead, the path opens out into a clearing with a thick tree in the middle. At its top is a network of planks and platforms built into the branches and a thick hanging rope connects the structure to the ground. Ally struggles free from Darryl's back and Chris hands over his crutches so that the four of them can approach and look upwards and then at each other to swear with delight.

THERE WAS ONCE THIS THING ON THE TELLY about a serial killer. That meant a man who was a murderer over and over and over again. The girl remembers that night she saw it – up late, on the couch barely blinking, hoping her mother wouldn't notice her or the lateness or the telly. This serial killer was interested in girls her own age, that time when people didn't call you a wee girl anymore but you weren't a teenager yet. Those were the girls he enjoyed.

The programme implied a mucky accompaniment to the murderings. Something to do with the girls' privates. She didn't understand it – not really – but it sewed her to the couch in a statue of horror. The difficult part was that she had to sit looking bored, just in case Mum glanced up and saw the girl and saw the time and saw what sort of programme it was that was on the telly.

She'd been given that abuse talk years and years ago. She knew a man might come up to you in the street while you were out and offer you the chance to go with him to see some kittens or get some sweets, then he would Take You Away. That was old news.

The only thing was, was that she thought it stopped there. The man would Take You Away, sort of like that old story about the bairns and the rats that went into the hill. The man would Take You Away, just to cheese off your mum and dad and then that would be it. There had been nothing up until that point – sitting stuck to the couch, back consciously straight, face consciously blank, telly light bleaching her eyes – nothing to suggest that someone, for mucky and unclear reasons, might have a strong desire to Take You Away and do something to your privates and then kill you.

And it wasn't that it might happen to her, the girl. It was that there were people alive on the planet that wanted to do that. They didn't want to go to the swimming pool or the pictures – they wanted to Take Girls Away and do terrible stuff to their privates instead. Or maybe it was that they did want to go swimming or watch a film and they would do all those normal things and at the same time also be really strongly wanting to Take Her Away.

Might be walking down Jimmy's Loan say, and might feel a breathing presence too close behind her, this warmth in the lane, and then feel a rough palm come around her head and grab her by the face. She'd never considered the possibility of that red palm descending over her eyes, which was how he did it, the serial killer. From behind, arm round the face. They showed you a re-enactment.

What happened to people that made them turn out like that? How did you end up all mixed up wrong when once you were a tiny baby, a thing that knew nothing, that was fresh and clean and that looked up at its mum or dad with trust? And a person like the serial killer still had that all gurgling away inside him. He had the baby version of him in there somewhere and was still able to do the things he did.

Then the programme was drawing to a close and it turned out they were keeping something back for the very end. It was what he did with the girls' bodies after he did the murders on them. That was the bit that left her perspiring in the dark, later, in bed, able to hear all the creaks and moans that people tell you are the house settling. She heard them as muscular fingers grasping at window latches, the face behind the glass leaving tusks of condensation on the pane. She was able to hear them as a heavy body beneath the bed, a body that snuck in when she was brushing her teeth and now lay beneath her. She was able to hear those creaks and moans as the creaks of ancient trees twisting in the wind and the moans of girls beneath them.

The murderer was a kind of park ranger in America and what he'd done with those pale fragile bodies – once he'd finished whatever mucky, unusual thing he ached to perform more than anything else – was he hid them beneath the trees in his park. He hid the girls in the dark spaces amongst the roots, in animal holes all gummed up with webs.

With the treehouse before her, she's getting memories of these girls coming back to her strong. She's seeing them down there in the black emptiness, seeing them crawl out like insects from a rock. Shivers once to dispel the image. The treehouse isn't like that, not at all. The trunk of the tree's like crocodile skin and has knots of puckered bark bleeding with honeyish trickles of sap.

Chris laughs. 'It's a proper den.'

Darryl wipes the hair from his brow. 'I heard it was amazing, but this is just ... Amazing.'

'Let's get on with it,' says Ally, circling the tree's roots. 'How am I meant to get up there anyway?'

'Here,' says Chris. 'That's a thing.'

The process involves Chris and Darryl climbing the rope first and the girl helping Ally to make a loop in the rope that he can put his foot in and be pulled up by. He doesn't speak the whole time, won't meet the girl's eye. Once he's up then it's the girl's turn. She holds the rope and faces the top, settles her feet and begins to yank herself upwards. If you lock your ankles and thighs together you can keep a grip on the rope and use your hands for pulling. About halfway up though she starts to get this feeling. It's a sort of pins-and-needles in her legs' bones. It's like stretching or going over a road bump in a fast car.

'Come on,' calls Chris. 'Get yourself up.'

By the time she's at the top she can feel her face is flushed. Ally's sitting in the middle of the platform, leaning on the trunk. 'You alright?' he squints.

'Aye,' she says. 'Fine.'

'You look funny,' he says.

'No.'

The treehouse is the kind of thing you read about in certain kinds of books from the library. The ones about rosy-cheeked English bairns that went on adventures and solved crimes and probably built boats and made you feel rubbish that you were just sitting on your arse reading the story. The floor's made of boards of wood and has low sides of milk crates tied together with orange twine. On the floor are seven beer bottles full of thick rainwater and bloated fag butts. There are some magazines over in the far corner that look like they might be those magazines for grown-ups – she doesn't go over to check. Behind

46

the top of the uppermost branches is the gigantic sky of towel-white clouds and over the way they've come you can make out the very tips of buildings above the trees.

Darryl kneels down behind one of the crates and aims an imaginary weapon over the side. 'It's even got bits for gunning down enemies,' he says, making the sound of a machine gun with his mouth.

'Alright,' says Ally. 'Enough pissing about. We need to do the official gang handshake.'

Chris finishes pulling the rope up and turns to look at him. 'What you on about?'

'You won't be able to do it,' Ally tells the girl. 'It's traditional.'

The girl shrugs.

'Eh?' says Chris. 'What's traditional?'

'The gang handshake.'

'Since when are we a gang?'

Ally gets himself up with a hand on the trunk behind him. 'We've always been a gang. Darryl, get over here and put your hand in.'

Darryl extends his hand towards Ally like he's waiting for it to be kissed. 'Like that?'

'That's it,' says Ally, shuffling closer. 'Now you,' he tells Chris.

Chris rests his hand on top of Darryl's and gives the girl this look of apology. Ally presses his fist into the others' hands before exploding it up into the air. 'Power of dragon!' he shouts.

Chris jerks his hand out of the handshake like it's been burned. 'The fuck was that?'

'Sorry,' Ally tells the girl. 'You probably didn't understand what was happening there. It's an old tradition and it didn't seem right to ignore it on your behalf.'

'It's fine,' she says. 'I'm not bothered.'

Darryl slaps his hands together. 'Right. What's the plan?'

'It might be difficult,' winces Ally. 'See, not everyone's played all the games.' He looks about himself as if he's not talking about anyone in particular.

'What games?' says the girl.

'Ally—' says Chris.

'Alright, alright. Have you played Half-time Harry?'

'Ally, *I've* never played Half-time Harry,' says Chris.

Darryl slaps his hands together again, oblivious to the argument going on about him. 'Got it,' he says. 'Truth or dare.'

Darryl hugs the trunk with wide-open arms. 'It's so bad,' he says.

'You've got to do it,' says Ally, cross-legged on the floor.

'I don't think I can. It's so minging.'

'It's the rules, mate,' laughs Chris, squatting on a crate. 'You've been dared.'

The girl laughs at the sight too – Darryl's arm span stupidly wide and him cringing at the smell and dirt of the tree.

'Go on,' says Ally. 'Show it some love.'

'Fuck,' Darryl whispers and he opens his mouth and places it over the tree's dusty wrinkles and moves his lips around while the rest count to five. When the countdown's over he recoils and wipes his mouth with the sleeve of his top.

'I just kissed a tree,' he says, a little teary.

'You're such a mink,' says Ally.

Ignoring the insult, Darryl crosses the boards and sits down among the group. 'Who's next?' he says, a fleck of bark sticking to the bottom of his smile.

'She is,' points Ally.

The girl feels all eyes on her. She's played truth or dare back home but none of their games ever involved someone kissing a tree.

'Not if she doesn't want to,' says Chris.

'Aye, she does,' says Ally.

'I can play,' she tells them.

She tries to imagine the worst dare she can think of, meaning the one they'll come up with. Sometimes at the school Abbie McMurdo or Lesley Philips would come up to you and get you to choose truth or dare while you ate your Hula Hoops and you'd say, 'Truth,' and then they'd ask you what was the matter with your mum.

'See,' says Ally. 'She can play. What'll we get her to do?'

'Get off with the tree,' says Darryl.

'We've done that,' says Ally.

'Aye,' says Chris. 'We've done that.'

What she could do is say her gran's wanting her back by a certain time and that she'll need to leave now if she's not going to get in deep shite. But she can imagine how those words would taste – sugary and just too babyish to even think about voicing.

Ally leans back. 'Well, anyway. Truth or dare?'

'Truth.'

All three go, 'Hm.'

'So,' says Ally. 'The way that we play with truths is that you have to do three of them.' He leans forward again, unable to get comfy on the boards. When he crosses his legs, he has to hold them down with his hands.

The girl nods in agreement and a disturbance in the trees off to the right sends up a cloud of birds.

'One each,' says Ally.

Darryl points at her. 'Where're you from?'

She gives them the name of her town and Ally groans. 'What a waste of a fucken question! You could ask that any time, not during truth or dare. Jesus, Darryl. Sometimes I wonder about you. Sometimes I wonder maybe you should be up the special school.'

'That was shocking,' agrees Chris, and Darryl's lip pouts.

'I know – how many folk have you got off with?' asks Ally and Chris makes a sound. Ally ignores him and keeps looking at the girl with his face of hunger.

'Three,' she says. That sounds like a safe bet.

Ally slaps his knee. 'Only three?'

'Aye,' she says. 'So what?'

'Try adding a zero to the end of that,' he says and points to his own chest.

'You've got off with *thirty* lassies?' says Chris. 'Since when? What lassies?'

'Hundreds of lassies. They all go to other schools. And it's been more than kissing, let me tell you.'

'Well, tell us then,' laughs Chris.

'Don't be such a sexist,' says Ally. 'You think I'm telling you about my lassies so you can tug-off about it later on?'

Chris does this great big exaggerated nod. 'Oh aye. I'm sure.'

'You're right to be sure! Some of the things I've done would put hairs on your chest, Chris my boy.'

'I've only got off with one lassie,' says Darryl forlornly.

'And to be fair mate,' says Chris, 'that was your cousin.'

'Aye,' agrees Ally, 'and at a barbecue as well.'

'But seriously,' says Chris. 'Thirty lassies, man. You're talking complete bollocks.'

Ally laughs. 'Don't get lippy with me, Christopher. Just cause you've never got off with anyone in your whole lonely lifetime.'

Chris bites his tongue. You can see he feels protective of Ally, probably because of whatever makes him use crutches, and yet Ally talks to him like that and Chris doesn't say a thing.

'Who were the three lads?' asks Darryl and everyone turns to her.

'Just these lads I knew back home,' she says. 'They were footballers and stuff.'

Chris scowls. 'Footballers?'

'Anyway,' says Ally. 'What's your truth? I'm wanting to get on with some proper dares, none of this lassie nonsense.'

Chris looks at the girl's feet. His lips open but there's no question within. He rubs his face. 'Shite.'

'What have I done to deserve a pal like you?' asks Ally, struggling to his feet. 'Forget it. Somebody dare me – I'm choosing dare. Don't even bother to ask, it's a dare for me. We've had plenty truths for one day and I'm sick to death with them to be honest.'

Darryl points to one of the beer bottles. 'Drink some of that.'

Ally scratches his head in anger. 'I'm obviously not drinking fucken manky old rainwater. Come on Darryl, do I look like I enjoy shitting poison out my arse? Dare me something proper.'

She barely has time to think before it falls from her mouth. 'Walk to the end of that branch and back,' she says and points to the thickest bough, stretching from under the platform and out into the open air.

The atmosphere changes. She's overstepped the mark.

51

Darryl draws in a breath through gritted teeth. 'Ooh,' he goes, his face lighting up from pleasurable fear.

Ally ignores him, nods with respect and says, 'Alright.' He hobbles over to the side of the platform. He uses his crutches to balance and everyone watches in silence. The girl's throat is thick with something. He shuffles along the branch, an inch at a time and they all swallow.

And then he's free of the platform. He reaches a bit where the branch kinks and as he goes to move upwards his body stutters.

His arms flap.

Out there on the branch you can see how delicate he is, how at odds his body is with his person. You can make out the kneecaps through his jeans and he's making little whimpers as he keeps balance. Chris is holding onto his own legs with nerves and rising to rush out and help. Another thick branch connects from above at the end of Ally's bough and he's reaching towards it with his crutch and wee wisps of his hair get tickled by the air.

Ally turns on his axis at the end of the bough. 'There,' he says. 'Told you.'

Chris and Darryl are cheering and clapping and so's the girl.

'There,' he says again, his voice muted by the wind. 'See?' Above his head the sky is split in four by a cross of vapour trails. He has each arm outstretched, the crutches jammed into the branches around.

'Come back in, mate,' says Chris.

Ally begins to make the crawl back along the branch. He takes one step forward, two, and then his foot slips, dislodging a handful of shredded bark. The girl sees it, the bark, cascade down the side and meander and swerve into the open. She sees Ally's foot move downwards,

52

jerking around for purchase and Darryl and Chris are rising and shouting and moving forwards to help and she can't stop seeing the fluttering shards of bark and Ally's foot spasming in empty air.

Chris scuttles out along the branch to pull Ally in and heave him onto the floor of the treehouse and she comes back into the present and goes over to check he's alright. What's wrong with her that she could sit there and watch falling bark?

She gets down beside him. 'Are you OK?'

Ally gulps down air as the adrenaline fades. He sits up and checks himself over. 'I'm fine,' he says. 'No thanks to you. But how about that, lads? Who's next?'

There's some talk about Darryl drinking the rainwater from one of the bottles, but in the end it doesn't happen. Instead, Ally dares him to spit up into the air and catch it in his own mouth.

That night she's in bed, trying to sleep. Muscles keening and hair heavy from dried sweat, she struggles to bring her body down from the path it's racing. Her mind plays her the day so she can watch her own performance – did she let the mask slip? Did the camera catch any glimpse of the softness within?

From her memory of the treehouse, she sees a bird career off into the centre of the sky until it disappears from view. As she looks into that bright whiteness, she thinks of the afternoon with Mum down at the water. The pond or loch or whatever she passed on the first morning with her grandparents. How good it felt to sit on the bank and let her feet be washed and rewashed by the water's shuddering movement, how she'd rolled off the bandage from her ankle, the ankle she'd hurt falling from the tree, and laid it out beside her. Let the cast bob. The sound of cars going past up on the road was kind of like bees.

'Are you being safe?' Mum called from the picnic benches.

'Aye,' she called back.

Later, with feet drying and the wine bottle close to empty, they took a bench each and lay down to sunbathe. They got that way where you're not dreaming yet but you can see pictures and hear sounds that aren't there.

Then Mum sat up and pointed. 'There's the bus,' she said. 'It's going.'

Sure enough – there was the bus pulling away from the lay-by up on the road.

'That's the last one I bet,' Mum said, leaning herself backwards onto the bench and giggling.

What's really sad is that she wasn't even upset or worried, because she believed her mother would know what to do. She wouldn't have let the last bus go without having a back-up plan. She cared about the girl more than anything else in the world and would die before she'd let her get stranded out in the countryside. She remembers asking Mum what they would do now that the bus had gone. She remembers Mum's head nodding in and out of sunlight, glares bleeding through the strands of her hair.

'Don't be so uptight,' she said. 'It'll all be alright on the night.'

'For definite?'

Mum reached across and they linked their pinkies together, which meant: Promise.

And then there was this other group down at the furthest away picnic table, throwing back booze the whole time and the sun's slow dive giving them this signal so that they started to shout and push each other and mess around in that hard way men sometimes did.

It grew cold enough down by the water that the girl started to wish she'd brought a jumper, or that someone had brought a jumper for her. The sun was gone and Mum was smoking fag after fag and the group down at the other table were maybe looking over and were maybe whistling. Mum peered at the girl over her fag's glowing tip and then climbed over the table to hold her face in her hands.

'You're going to be gorgeous when you grow up.'

The girl said, 'Thanks.'

She wanted to ask what they were going to do but couldn't risk Mum losing her temper. Behind her, up on the road, cars went past.

'Could we phone for a lift?' she said.

'Did I ever tell you about my best pal?' Mum asked. 'My very best wee pal? We had such a riot at the school. Me and her and this lad Stig. We used to get up to all sorts.'

The same sort of birds appeared, flying low over the water, quarrelling and birling within and around each other. Maybe this was what reminded her ... Her mother is going, 'Did I ever tell you about my best wee pal?' as the cars going past up on the road dwindle and men's voices are growing and her mother's face is made black by the sun setting behind her.

'What was her name though?' says Mum. 'I can't quite remember ... Her name? Her ... second name?' She clicks her fingers beneath the table. 'Was it Carmichael?'

'I don't know, Mum.'

'Carpenter! It was Carpenter. Or was it?'

'Alright darling?' shouts a voice from the furthest picnic table.

Mum's head's in her hands and she's rubbing her temples and clenching her teeth. She's saying, 'Fuck,' over and over, and then she's up like a shot and storming along the pathway to the road. The men are booing and the girl doesn't know if her mother's even aware of them. She follows and finds her leaning against the bus shelter.

'Are you alright?'

'I think it was Carpenter, but it's hard to remember. Listen: how are we going to get back? That was the last bus, you know? I don't know what you were thinking of taking so long in the water.'

The light's escaping them now and the girl can't quite make out the group down by the furthest bench unless she squints as a car passes and she's able to make them out for a moment – bright pulses of illuminated and dancing male bodies. Her mother's sobering up now. They hold hands and try to hitchhike and Mum shows the Vs to any car that ignores them.

Her jaw's trembling. 'Jesus,' she says. 'Why were you in the water so long?'

The girl doesn't answer, just watches back along the road for the sweep of headlights a few hills over.

Not a single car stops.

'We've got lifts coming in a minute if you're needing one,' said a voice from behind them. It belonged to a man with a white T-shirt and shaved head, swaying from an afternoon's drinking in the sun.

The girl felt her mother relax, her hand going slack in her own. She put some of her hair behind an ear. 'Aye. Aye – that'd be great.'

The car they drove in went too fast. If the girl craned her head over and looked in the front she could see the needle go up to eighty, ninety. As the driver pulled the car around corners the girl was pressed into either the door or the man beside her. Her mother was up front, laughing at whatever the driver was saying. She closed her eyes and could smell the drink on all of them and the reek coming from the armpit just beside her head.

'Aw, you're a filthy bastard,' she heard her mother laugh.

She was going to ask them in, the girl could feel it. Mum'll ask them where they're off to now and then say it's so late and they should just come back to hers for a can or two.

She could feel the words coming from her mother's mouth as she spoke them.

All the men nodded and said, 'Aye, alright,' and they came home with them and stayed up past when the girl fell asleep and she could hear their shouting and drinking through her bedroom door.

Her usual routine in the morning before school was that she would eat her cereal in the living room and watch telly. The morning after the day at the water there were men sleeping all over the couch and armchair. There were crumpled cans on the floor and little saucers filled with ash and butts. She ate her cereal in the kitchen and brushed her teeth and dressed in silence. All across her bedroom ceiling were glow-in-the-dark stars and planets but in the morning they were dull and green. The water had got in underneath her cast and you could feel the flesh there was tingling. She found a pen and jammed it down the side.

You pull back hard enough on the slats and in time they'll come. Hard though – *hard* hard. You need to be basically horizontal in the air with your trainers pushing against the fence slat either side of the one you're hanging off and you need to be jerking yourself backwards with all your might so that the nails connecting the fence to its bars wriggle themselves loose. You'll go flying when it comes though. You'll land right on your arse in the dirt. You'll have some splinters in your palms but you'll have torn that fence to pieces if you do it enough times.

Chris is better than the girl at this. He's stronger and taller and his efforts have more persistent force behind them. Chris tears off three slats for every one she can. After he tears them off he smashes them against the rubble and washing machines lying about them in the wasteground so that the slats shatter into long fibrous chunks. He drives some of the pieces into the earth and others he frisbees up into the sky. He watches the girl as he destroys.

Or another technique is that you can be like Darryl and have jumped over the fence and be kicking the slats down from the other side in a frenzy of violence. You can be running towards the fence and flying with your foot outstretched or turning away from the fence and hammering your heel into it backwards so that the chosen slat gets shunted forwards.

'Fuck you,' he's shouting as he's kicking against the fence, lost in the madness.

Ally sits over there on an upturned wheelie bin and kills himself laughing. He's not up to breaking the fence himself, but it's his laughing and his shouts of, 'Yes! Finish it!' that power the whole enterprise. He claps when one of them pulls a slat off – the others pile them up beside him so he can rest his little trainer there like an explorer with his foot proud atop a bullet-filled animal corpse.

'That fence's laughing at you, mate,' he tells Darryl. 'It's calling your mum a tart.'

Darryl kicks a slat in its middle and his foot bursts through and both ends snap up and down.

'Yes!' shouts Ally. 'You killed it.'

'You're a machine,' says Chris.

Darryl doesn't respond, just keeps kicking and smashing. He's got stamina that boy. You can't ever imagine him running out of breath or getting a stitch so bad that he has to stop and lean over with hands on knees. He's able to fire up the rope at the treehouse in three or four long leaps.

'Rah!' he shouts and splinters his foot through another board.

She's sweating from the work. When she licks her top lip, she tastes the juice from before. It tastes of chemicals and pineapples. There's not another beating heart around

59

for half a mile. No houses overlook the wasteground and you could do whatever you wanted out here and no one would see. Likewise, you could get your ankle trapped under some rubble or a dark figure could materialise and throttle you and no one would know. If there's a place like this back home then she's never been there. She sticks to back gardens with Fiona and Raymond and they're often too scared to go further than the smallest park.

The girl wipes sweat from her forehead with her wrist and attacks the fence again. All the wood is bleached from years and years of sun and rain. Same colour as driftwood except it's got these bleeding brown wounds all along it which are the nail heads leaking their rust down the boards. When the slat she's working on gives way it cracks in half rather than coming off completely. She chucks the half she's holding over towards Ally and climbs back up.

She's hanging off this next slat, hoping she doesn't slip and let her bare ankle fall into the bed of nettles lurking at the fence's base. You just have to look at those evil weeds to feel your skin prickle. It's not even the sting that would be the worst bit. The worst bit would be having to keep going with the pulling off of the fence slats with this huge red rash on your ankle but not be able to tend to it, because no doubt in that scenario the boys would laugh at you and say you were a typical lassie.

Same thing happened the other day at the treehouse. She was going down the rope, lowering herself with crossed feet and hands, when she lost the grip on her feet and went off sliding and had to use her hands to stop herself and she slid all the way to the bottom and the rope felt alive from fire.

At the bottom she looked and saw her hands were raw and bleeding.

'You alright?' Chris shouted from above.

'Aye,' she said, dusting her palms on the arse of her jeans and regretting it.

Once the fence is as smashed up as it's going to be, Chris and Darryl load all the fractured chunks of wood into a wheelbarrow that's rusted to the colour of a satsuma and trundle it over to the bottom of the wasteground. There's no plan, no endgame. It's just smash up the fence and move it around. Everyone hurls their glass juice bottles against the remainder of the fence before they go. All the bottles explode and they're like see-through fireworks.

The middle of the wasteground's a very slight hill. The girl looks back the way they've come and sees the entrance way far off in the distance. The only living things here are nettles and weeds that grow up among the old bikes and bricks and broken machinery. The three boys are already descending, the wheelbarrow screeching like a bag of mice as it's rolled along, so she hurtles after them, prancing off rocks.

Down at the other end of the wasteground is the old factory wall. Just this one solitary wall jutting up from the rubbled floor like a ship in the ocean. It has lines of sticking-out bricks, which were once floors and walls when the factory existed. On the side facing them are white, person-tall letters that say:

ALLUMS OF WEST RO

They go round the factory wall into the area that would once have been the factory's insides. This is where they dispose of the broken fencing. They pick the pieces from the wheelbarrow and throw them mindlessly around. There's a huge coil of metal rope with bars knotted up

61

within. Darryl spends a good chunk of time trying to pry the metal coil apart wide enough that Chris can get his hand in and pull out the metal bars. He tries for so long his fingers and palms become blistered.

It doesn't matter though because when you go over the pile of rubble behind the coil of metal rope there's this entire other section with more of the metal bars all lined up neat waiting for you like presents. A good game is to use the metal bars like swords or just to batter your weapon off the side of the factory wall so that the wall spits out clouds of pink dust that make you sneeze.

The girl grabs a bar and goes against Darryl in a sword-fight. They square up and start slowly, glancing their bars off each other's, making slicing sounds with their mouths. They act like knights, forcing off their opponent's sword with exaggerated yells and swinging the bars in the air. Darryl pretends the girl's bar has pierced his stomach and he goes onto the rubble, crying and moaning and begging for his life. The girl stands above him and holds out her bar.

'No mercy!' says Ally.

She brings the sword down slow onto Darryl's neck and she cuts his head off, clean. Darryl screams, clawing at his throat, making Chris and Ally laugh. She mimes cleaning his blood off on her jeans and pretends to shovel earth over him – a shallow grave.

Also in this section of what used to be the factory is a tramp den – two sleeping bags lined up beside each other and a tiny dump of Super Lager cans and balled up newspaper and crisp packets. You can see a patch of blackened rock where fires have been started and there are a few groceries stored within a metal box.

All of you stand at the crest of the rubble pile and look

down at the den. Between the two sleeping bags is a tiny white puck: a single candle. You can see the two of them, these two men, who were once young themselves and probably rampaged around wastegrounds of their own, not even considering the possibility that they might be the sort of bairns who would grow up and become old and have to sleep out like that with just a single candle for warmth or comfort. They were probably old-fashioned little boys who wore thick wool shorts and had haircuts like grown men.

The three boys shout and fall upon the den and raze it to the ground. The sleeping bags get filled with cans and beaten to mulch with metal bars. Ally throws the candle as hard as he can against the factory wall. One of them finds a carton of chunky green milk and squeezes it out and smears it over everything. The smell it gives off is unreal but they still pick up the sleeping bags and run, trailing them behind in the air like flags.

The girl laughs and whoops and claps. She doesn't destroy anything in the den herself but she drives the others on. After it's over she forgets about it, and it's not when she's home in bed that she remembers, like you'd expect. It's the next day when she's watching telly and there's an advert on where this rich guy doesn't use the right sort of credit card or something and through magic he's turned into a homeless guy with the open-toed boots and bindle and everything. The girl swallows and gets this picture of the sleeping bags' flapping polyester, damp and broken from the cans inside. The two men come back from where they've been and they see the mess and they sit down on the piles of rubble. They can smell the rotten milk too – it's sharp and sour and a little bit sweet.

THE TOWN SQUIRMS WITH THE BUSY JOY of a long summer. Weekdays, the girl goes with her gran and gets to know shopkeepers. Men in aprons look up from ledgers and smile when they enter, door chiming, and the girl wonders what kind of storybook planet she's washed up on. Whatever they do, they're finished by lunch, so the girl can speed-eat her food going from foot to foot and telling her grandparents, 'Thanks' between mouthfuls and be out the door and feeling the itchy blanket of the sun's mid-day peak. She ferrets out the boys by sound and taste – by cocking her ear to the cackles and roars of plans or breathing in woodfires and aerosol deodorant. They call her Stretch now because she's tall for her age. Alright Stretch? one of them'll say when she climbs into their midst over fence or through hedge.

Some mornings aren't shopping, they're seeing Gran's friend. The girl drinks a can of juice and watches Gran and her cronies talk about everyone they ever knew who died. They drink weak tea and talk about Ailsa Doherty who drowned off the Costa Brava and Jennie Campbell who sat in a chair for four months before the fire brigade burst the door down with axes and Jennie Campbell had to be siphoned from the house.

The girl's grandmother tells them that her Alec never had a friend in the world, work and family not counting. The girl thinks of her grandfather, looking up at her from inside the shed, his face dusted in powdered wood.

'Never a friend in the world,' confirms her grandmother.

'Alright Stretch?' says Chris. Patches of freckles have begun to blossom under each of his eyes.

'Alright,' she says and sits down cross-legged. 'What's going on?'

He points towards Ally and Darryl, on hands and knees scraping at an area of shredded grass with trowels. 'Digging a hole.'

Ally leans back on his haunches, out of breath, saying it's useless, but Darryl keeps going. Ally gets to his feet and scrambles his crutches up beneath him. 'Where've you been?'

'Had to go out with my gran,' she says.

He considers her closely. 'Aye?'

'Aye.'

Darryl holds up a white curled piece of something. 'You reckon that's a worm or a root?' he asks.

Ally glances back to him with a glare of distaste.

It's agreed by everyone: treehouse.

But what they find there throws their plans into turmoil, because all along the pathway mushrooms have been blasted to smithereens. Pale flakes of them litter the earth and larger chunks hang from low branches and thickets.

Darryl wonders was it wolves that done it? And then up at the treehouse someone's tied this plastic willy to the end of the climbing rope and sprayed paint on the side of the tree. The four of them stand back and consider the menace.

Darryl wails, 'What's going on?'

Ally's eyes flick to slits and to Darryl he goes, 'This is all your fault.'

'How's it Darryl's fault?' asks Chris.

Ally reminds Chris about the time Darryl wiped a full palmful of snot down the side of Big Dave Storey's dirt bike and how he was seen doing it and Big Dave Storey and his mates chased them over five streets' worth of gardens and how Ally had to hide in a coal shed and one of his crutches got snapped in half and that's how come he got the new ones in the first place.

'Oh right,' nods Chris. 'Aye. That might be it, Darryl.'

The girl tries not to look at the rotating thingummy on the rope. 'Who's Dave Storey?' she asks.

'Like the hardest guy you've ever seen,' says Chris. 'He drank a goldfish once. He used to bully Ally loads when he was still at the school.'

'No he never,' says Ally. 'We were actually pretty good mates until this clown blew his beak on the bike.'

Chris asks what sort of mate it was that called you a mongo with his face right up close to yours in the play-ground at the top of his voice or that jabbed you hard in the stomach with a badminton racket so that you were winded and had to sit out PE?

Ally tuts. 'It was all banter, Stretch. I gave as good as I got.'

Darryl, walking back and forth with his palms on the small of his back, looking oddly housewife-ish, says, 'Oh man. I'm going to get my head kicked in.'

'I wouldn't be surprised if you do,' says Ally. 'I wouldn't be surprised if you get your head kicked in any day now.'

Chris cuts the thingummy down with his Spanish penknife and it lands with a hollow dunk. Ally kicks it away and it rolls, settles against a knot of root and regards them. She climbs the rope so fast that she gives herself more rope burns. The treehouse floor has been baked hot and they gaze out over the woods, watching for villains. All the girl can see is the thin wall of vapour rising from the dual carriageway.

They find a spot among the trees on the far side of the clearing and climb inside to wait. The girl crouches, arms wrapped around her shins. Darryl sits with legs crossed, plucking his raw bottom lip while Chris and Ally alternate between peering out under their palms and lying on their fronts. Ally's wrapped a string of ivy around his crutches and drawn black stripes beneath his eyes. It's close in there, among the breathing plants and her T-shirt clings to her back.

They wait and wait. Darryl opens a can of juice with a hiss and is scowled at. Later on, he points towards a broken branch. 'Could be a sign of forced entry,' he says and Chris tells him not to be daft.

'Here,' whispers the girl. 'What if we just pack this in?'

'Classic lassie's logic there,' says Ally, peering at the clearing beneath his palm. 'We need to reclaim the area or our dignity's been compromised.'

Ally and Darryl start to argue about the best system for supreme victory. Should they go and seek out Dave Storey and his mates or maintain their position in the woods?

'You're full of shite anyway, Ally,' says Darryl. 'If we did manage to find them, it's not like you'd even do anything.'

'Are you calling me a coward?' asks Ally. 'This coming from the lad who wouldn't cross a field that didn't even have a cow in it, in the end?'

Chris asks her if she fancies going for a wander, and she tells him, 'Aye.'

'See you in a bit,' he tells the others. 'Me and Stretch are going to do some recon.'

They nip across the clearing, past the tree, and into the woods on the far side.

'Pair of fannies,' says Chris, coming up behind her and whacking at things with a stick.

The girl looks to the side as she talks, to let her voice carry. 'Who are? Them two?'

'Aye,' says Chris. 'They can be a right couple of bairns sometimes.'

The girl nods to the path before her.

'Sorry he's giving you a hard time,' he adds. 'He's just scared.'

A river of thick mud pools by the path. They jump over it and then back again.

'So what's it like back home?' he asks. 'What's your mum like?'

'She's got this mad, crazy job. She has to work all day – all night sometimes – and she doesn't like to leave me. That's how come I'm staying here.' Her brain lies for her, she doesn't even need to make it up.

'Aye?'

'Aye. She works in the city, in banks and so on. In businesses.'

'Wow,' says Chris. 'That must be cool. My big brother

68

works in businesses. We don't see him much anymore because of it.'

And after that there's a minute of not-talking, where they stand nearby to each other and are looking this way and that, and then Chris says, 'So,' to her, and she can see his eyes are peering right over.

'So,' she goes.

As they're walking they hear shouts from somewhere off to the left: male yells of anger, or pleasure. Shouts coming from the hidden depths of the woods, ringing back and forth. They run to the clearing to find Ally and Darryl lying on their fronts.

'Did you hear that?' pants Chris. 'That shouting?'

'Negatory,' says Ally. 'What did it sound like?'

Chris scowls. 'What did it sound like? It sounded like shouting.'

'Did it sound like it was Dave Storey shouting?' asks Darryl, twisting around.

'I don't know what he shouts like.'

Darryl nods. 'Hm.'

They redouble their efforts, keeping extra still and watching hard for any signs of the Storey gang.

They see nothing but birds and make their way home in disgrace.

'Christ Alec, come here,' says her grandmother, grabbing her grandad by the hips and pulling up his jacket to show the untucked shirttails.

'It's fine,' he grunts. 'It's not like you can see it.'

He rolls his eyes to the girl as his wife jerks the shirt down into his trousers. She covers her mouth so Gran doesn't spy her smile.

The doorbell goes. 'Oh, there's Karen,' says Gran, toddling down the hallway.

Grandad does this slow turn on the living room rug. 'What's she got me trussed up in this for?' he asks. 'It's only Barbara's.'

Karen comes into the room and just like that it's all brighter. She gives off this ... something, this lightness, that draws eyes to her. 'Look at you Mr Ross!' she exclaims. 'Aren't we looking smart?'

Grandad nods. 'Am I gorgeous?'

'Oh absolutely,' says Karen, slumping into the couch beside the girl. 'Wouldn't you say so?'

'I'm getting a big head,' he says.

Gran comes in and gives him a once over, checking for creases or stray hairs on his jacket. He's pulling these faces to Karen and the girl and they're giggling at his mugging. All of them go out into the hallway and she can hear them discuss emergencies and when they'll be back from Barbara's.

She lets her attention wander to the wall of photographs across from her. There's all the ones of younger grandparents and dogs and people she doesn't know. And then there's the one of her mother: Mum, a man, and a baby. And then it's obvious – of course. The baby's her, her newborn face as red and angry as raw salmon, and as wet too.

She goes across the room and listens to the chatter from the hallway. She unhooks the frame from the wall and sits down on the couch with it, right on the edge of the cushion so she can fly over and put it back when she hears Karen coming. They must be in a hospital because Mum's wearing one of those gowns. She's sweaty and the camera's gone off just as she's moving her head so her features are blurred and expressionless.

What she can't take her eyes off is her mother's hand

– the one not holding the girl. You can see it appearing round the other side of the man and it's clawing onto the fleece and possibly flesh of his hip with this mad strength like she's about to tip sideways off of the bed.

She brings the frame up close and the back of it comes loose in her hand, letting the photo itself slip free. It lands in the girl's lap and the three of them are obscured by a hazy white reflection. She turns it over. On the back someone's written: *Angie, Pete, Chloe*, and a date which is her birthday. Flips it again to see the baby's red skin shining in the camera's flash and if you look close you can see the tiny expression of fury on the little face. A pressure is building inside the girl and she's starting to slip, so she gets the photo back onto the wall.

She doesn't look at Karen when she comes back through and throws herself down on the couch. She's too much to look at all at once, so the girl keeps her eyes trained on the telly instead. There's a programme on where a load of people go skydiving. She can feel Karen watch her. Manages to avoid it for only so long before she cracks and takes a peek at Karen out the corner of her eye. She laughs at the face Karen's pulling, this big daft gurn.

'Awright darling?' Karen grunts.

'Hiya,' says the girl.

Karen stops pulling the face. 'I've been looking forward to this. A proper girls' night in.'

The girl nods and then doesn't know what to say, so goes back to the telly. When Karen leans forward her top slides over her love handles, these sweet tanned curves, and the girl gets knives of guilt from comparing her to Mum, who's all skin and bones and ribs.

'Aw,' says Karen, 'is this that one where they push folk out of planes? It's horrible, eh? But funny, in a bad way.'

They watch together for a while and the girl relaxes into Karen being beside her and then, despite the badness, they're killing themselves, sort of crying from it.

'You shouldn't laugh,' says Karen.

The popcorn's still hot from the microwave but Karen throws a piece of it up into the air and catches it in her mouth.

'What do you want to be when you grow up?'

The girl panics and tells her a vet.

'I hate animals. See this?' Karen rolls up her jeans to show a scar on her calf. 'Dog bite. I was going to be an actress, did you know that? It's all bollocks though. I never did the end of year show for the college and that's part of your mark.'

'How come?'

'Just the rest of them, they were total fakers. I know how that sounds cause that's all acting is. See and there was this whole other thing with him,' she flicks her head towards the ceiling, 'and he never liked me doing it. The lads at the college ... Christ. I don't know. Sorry.'

The girl looks at the popcorn. 'What do you mean?'

Karen sucks on her lips. 'It's complicated.'

'OK,' says the girl.

Karen's brought down a toolbox only it's not tools inside, it's all the nail polishes she owns. They open the box and Karen picks some bottles and lays them out on the rug. There's bottles with redness and pinkness and blackness inside. Karen asks the girl what one she'd like and she picks the colour most like a shell. To do it properly, Karen must hold the girl by the hand. She grips her and pulls her wrist so that her fingers splay out and she lays the brush on each nail, sweeping this pearlish colour over every one. You can smell the polish filling the room – this rich fruit-flavour and sweets. Then it's the girl's turn to take Karen's fingers, hold them stiff, and paint with the same one she chose. She makes a mess of most of them, colouring in the cuticles too, but one or two aren't bad. They have to hold their hands up for drying, shaking them now and then and blowing. After the polish, you put on something clear for added shining and protection and then do the whole drying thing again, waggling your fingers and feeling the fresh cold.

'Show me,' says Karen.

The girl puts out her hand.

'Not bad,' says Karen. 'You can wash them in hot water to get rid of the rough edges.'

The girl moves the nails across her eyes and each one's like something precious, like a chunk of jewel. They put their hands together so they can compare.

She's got this craving to crawl over the couch and dig her way into Karen's brains, to see what she's seen. She wants to rummage amongst the memories and wear them like jewellery. In the future, she's looking at herself in the mirror and she's old and been to college and had boyfriends, like Karen. She's walking along and there's music playing and these sort of flowers grow up like magic.

Her grandfather comes home drunk. As her grandmother thanks Karen and presses notes into her hand, he sings sweetly in the kitchen. He comes through with his glasses off and his eyes looking tiny and deep. He slow dances with the girl on the rug and says into her ear with a bitter smelling voice that she's just like him.

73

'The pair of us,' he whispers. 'We're nothing like the rest of them.'

You can hear the front door go and then her grandmother bustles back in.

'Look at the state of him!' she says. 'How many whiskies was that?'

But she's laughing as he starts to slow dance with her instead. She says that he's awful and holds onto him by the braces. They tell the girl which CDs to play from the collection in the sideboard and they're all men with deep, warbling voices, singing about the war alongside soft pianos.

Her grandparents waltz across the rug in the unclear haze of just the lamps and you can see how long that love's been in this world.

'It's your mum,' says Gran's voice in the darkness.

She rubs her eyes and Gran pulls her dressing gown tighter at the bust and gestures the phone towards the girl until she sits up to take it.

On the other end is wet breath.

'Hello,' says the girl.

Long seconds pass. What time is it? Near five?

'Sweetie,' says the voice.

'Hiya Mum.'

Something dozy about her mother's voice, something missing. 'Sweetie,' it says again. 'What are you doing?'

'Nothing.'

A wheeze. 'Aye, I suppose so. Listen. You get to your bed, OK?'

'I'm in my bed,' says the girl and the wet breath clicks into dial tone. Gran is watching from the doorway and is looking so sad.

She remembers once, at home, lying in the dark and pretending to sleep as her mother crept in and there was this far-away tinkling sound. It was like fairies or angels or Santa. When she woke up the next day there were coins missing from her piggy bank. But her mother's fading out now. Everything else – Karen, the boys, Gran and Grandad – they're coming through in so many colours and so many sizes that there's just no room left.

'TODAY'S THE LAST OF THIS NONSENSE,' says Chris. 'If Dave Storey doesn't show up then I'm packing in all the army stuff.'

'And then what?' says Ally. 'Just go about our business like sitting ducks?'

'Maybe they weren't even looking for Darryl,' says Chris. 'It might have been like random.'

Darryl opens his eyes a bit.

'Excuse me if I don't think that's right,' says Ally.

They kill an hour or two messing around in the hiding spot and taking turns as lookouts. Chris uses his penknife to whittle a fallen branch into a kind of pointed spear. Ally gives him a look, suspicious of pretension. They play a game of imaginary battles.

'My go,' says Darryl, from down on the floor. 'Stretch. Would you rather be a bear that has to fight a lion, or a lion that has to fight a man?'

She thinks about it. 'The lion fighting the man.'

'Aye, OK, but the man has a gun.'

She laughs. 'Well if you're adding rules, then the bear.'

'The lion's got two heads though.'

It's hard to tell with Darryl whether he's being serious or not with the things he says.

'What a stupid fucken question,' says Ally. 'Obviously a lion would beat a man, gun or not. A lion's an apex predator, it's got fangs of death.'

'Right,' says Darryl. 'Well what would win out of a velociraptor – the ones in the kitchen in *Jurassic Park* – and a rhino?'

Ally spits with fury. 'Of course the velociraptor. Absolutely of course. They're the greatest hunter God ever dreamed up. Have you seen them claws?'

'But what about the rhino's horn?' says Darryl.

Ally gives him this long look, then says, 'You're living in a dream world, my friend.'

She squats in the bushes, far enough away so that the boys won't hear, hiking her jeans and knickers down around her ankles. As she goes, she wonders what they're saying about her back in the hiding place.

Amazing, they're maybe saying, how she's a lassie but still able to keep up with us lads.

But, I mean, that's not to say that she's doesn't still possess a certain feminine charm, Chris maybe interjects. That's the thing about her – you're getting the best of both worlds – and have you seen that nail polish?

Then: voices, out in the clearing.

There's nothing to wipe with so she pulls jeans and kickers up as one and creeps to the edge of the trees. Her belly flips. Chris and Ally and Darryl are huddled at the base of the tree and there's all these older lads standing around them. She can't make out what's being said but she can tell from his body language that Ally's trying to act casual. He's leaning on one crutch and flapping his hand. She kneels and moves around the circumference of the clearing to be able to hear better.

There's one lad standing ahead of the rest of them. He's tall and broad and his arse is fat, round. This must be the Dave Storey she's heard so much about. He jabs Ally in the chest, sharp, and Ally stumbles. There's another three older lads behind Dave Storey, one of them sitting low on a BMX. Another has rank wispy sideburns and that one snorts as Ally backs away from the poke.

'What is it yous're even doing out here?' says Storey, holding his arms out. 'Is this where yous come to shag each other?'

'No way,' says Ally, as Chris and Darryl shake their heads. 'Nothing like that going on here, Dave.'

'You'd better not be,' says Storey. 'We fucken hate poofters.'

He walks in a line before the three boys and the clearing is silent except for the slow rattle of the lad trying to ride his BMX over roots and mud.

'So what is it then, if yous arnae shagging each other?' asks Storey.

Chris and Darryl look to Ally, who swallows. 'Aw, you know, this and that. Football mostly – play a bit of footie.'

Storey turns to his mates and kills himself laughing. 'How's this one meant to play football?' he says, pointing at Ally's crutches. 'The fucken mongo.'

She gets sickness when he says the word. He spits it out like saliva – you see it make contact with Ally and he flinches, before trying to laugh along.

Storey and the BMX one and the lad with sideburns all become quiet. 'What's so fucken funny?' asks Storey. 'Are you laughing at me?'

'Naw,' says Ally. 'That isn't how it is, Dave. We're all mates here.'

'I'm not your fucken mate,' says Storey.

Chris is sort of stepping away from them. He's saying, 'We should be getting down the road.'

'Valente!' says Storey. 'Are you too good to hang about with us? Is that it?'

Chris chuckles, keeps eyes on ground.

'Valente here thinks he's too good for us,' says Storey and his mates make a grumble of disapproval. 'Anyway. Enough pissing about. I'm no here to talk to a mongo about football. It's you I'm interested in, Buchanan,' he says, rounding on Darryl.

Darryl says something too low for the girl to pick up.

'Never mind that,' says Storey. 'Be a man. Stick up for yourself. I thought you were some solid gangster, messing up my bike like?'

He begins to shadow-box in front of them, prancing left and right, throwing feints at all three. Each of the boys flinch as Storey's fist comes towards them.

Could she run out, make a distraction? Try and reason with this Storey? The three boys look tiny out in the clearing, these huge lads circling them. But there's no time, because already Storey's stopped.

'Fucken pathetic. Not worth my time. C'mere,' he says, holding a hand up to Darryl. 'No hard feelings?'

Darryl goes to extend his hand but before he can raise it past chest-height, Storey lunges forward and slaps him across the head and Darryl crumbles into the earth with a shriek. Storey leans right over Darryl and knuckles his face.

'Stay the fuck away from my bike, alright?'

'Alright,' says Darryl.

'Help your boyfriend then,' he tells Chris and Ally and he moves towards them like a punch is coming. Ally drops a crutch and all of them laugh and they lumber across the clearing and down onto the path. She's sure they're going to spot her as they pass, but she manages to go unnoticed. It's only then that she feels the air rushing through her.

Darryl's eye is red and thick and his face shines from sweat and emotion. He moans on the ground as Chris and Ally lean over.

'That looks like a nasty one, mate,' says Chris.

'I know,' says Ally. 'I was *this* close to getting one myself. Luckily Storey's got a lot of respect for me.'

They look over their shoulders as she approaches.

'Oh,' says Ally. 'Here she is.'

'Are you OK?' she asks Darryl.

'Ngh,' he says.

There's even something questioning in Chris. 'Where were you?' he says.

'I had to go for a pee,' she says.

'A pee,' says Ally. 'That's very convenient that is. A likely tale.'

'I did,' she says.

'We all wanted to go for pees,' says Ally, 'but some of us have a little thing called decency among comrades.'

'Mgh,' says Darryl.

'Were you hiding?' asks Chris.

'No,' she says.

'She was so hiding,' says Ally, flapping his crutches.

80

'She was hiding out like the traitor that she is. I knew this would happen. I mean, not this specifically, but I knew she was trouble – ever since she grassed.'

'I wasn't hiding,' she says. 'I went for a pee in the woods and then they came.'

'Grh,' says Darryl.

'It's maybe best if you went back,' says Chris. 'We need to see to Darryl.'

'Aye,' says Ally. 'Go on – get. That's the last time we trust a grass.'

Across the clearing and into the trees she keeps her pace nonchalant, counting her trainers' sounds on the forest floor. Once she's obscured, she breaks into a run, and Ally's voice is calling something wicked after her. The camera she floats ahead catches how she's not crying, how she's holding it together in the lens' glare.

She isn't crying, she isn't crying, she isn't crying.

That night and the next day she matches her grandad for silence – her grandmother says it's like living in a bleeding waxworks. Next day's the Saturday and she kills it reading in the room and she has tea with her grandparents and they watch all the usual Saturday stuff and the girl doesn't even care when the folk on telly win their prize or when all their dreams come true.

Upstairs, Karen is having a row with her man. You can't hear the details but it's nasty. Doors slam and they scream. The girl remembers cupboard doors slamming at home and she remembers cars roaring off down the road, leaving a silence, punctured by her mother's angry laughter. She would see people fight at the school – a girl's fist raised with a clump of wet hair held within. Once a boy's tooth flew through the sky. Someone pushed him and his jaw connected with an iron railing. Remembering Darryl's slap and the way he fell sends a shiver of something down her belly.

The girl stays underwater in the bath until her chest burns. When you twist to the side you can be completely submerged and when you break the surface you can hear Karen weep in the bathroom above. A round loch forms in her belly button when she pushes her stomach out and her skin goes pale beneath the water.

She spends next morning out in the heat – aimless.

An old man in a parka and red stubble stumbles by.

'Cheer up, son,' he tells the girl. 'Might never happen.'

When she gets to the post office they've nothing left in the penny mix except foam shrimps and white mice. She wanders down a garden path after a noise, but it's just some wee ones playing with a hose. A little boy with a mohican puts his thumb over the nozzle and sprays a sheet of water over the girl. She gives him the Vs.

Back at her grandparents' she finds Karen out on her step, smoking in a dressing gown.

'What's that?' she asks. 'Shrimps? Amazing, thanks.'

The girl sits on the step below.

'What's your plan for today then? Where's that lot that I usually see you going about with?'

The girl stretches a shrimp out as long as her arm before it snaps in two. 'Oh them? Don't know.'

Karen gives her a quizzical look.

'See, I dunno if I'm that into hanging about with them. They're a bit immature.'

Karen claps. 'A lassie after my own heart.'

They sit and share the bag of shrimps and the girl's thinking of the argument.

'Aye,' Karen says. 'A lassie after my own heart. You won't make the same mistakes as us lot, with blokes and that. You'll be alright.'

The girl nods – she doesn't know.

'Had a huge row last night,' says Karen, leaning into her. 'Bad one like. I told him, I said, I want you out. And so he went.'

She shakes her head and sniffs.

It's a right tip inside. There's a lot of opened CD cases and ashtrays and posters of bands on the walls. A rat runs in a wheel. Karen puts on the stereo and music begins mid-song.

'You'll love this one,' she says, curling up on the couch.

It smells of maleness in there, of men's toiletries and clothes. The girl knows it well enough from the bathroom at home, when Mum's pals were around, and the faintest traces of it on Chris and Darryl too. She perches on the wicker chair across from Karen. Despite the mess there's something about the room that makes it appealing. She's peering into a life she's yet to live. Karen gets up a few times to change the song on the stereo. She picks up a CD case from on top and turns it to the girl.

'This is his,' she says. 'Joni Mitchell. I bet you'd like her actually. Wanting it?'

The girl catches the thrown case. 'What happened?' she asks, holding up the CD.

Karen cocks her head left and right. 'Eh ... You wouldn't understand.'

She wishes Karen would give her a chance because she's desperate to know about it, desperate to see how life will be. Will she have her own place once she's Karen's age? Will there be a rat running in a wheel? Will friends and boyfriends be in her place, staying near for as long as she needs?

'Did you not like him anymore?' the girl asks.

'He was fine,' says Karen. 'It was just much more difficult than it needed to be.'

'Did he annoy you?'

Karen laughs. 'I probably annoyed him, if anything.'

The girl wonders if she'll look out of windows to see streetlights in darkness and of course moons and stars. She wonders if her bed will be large and comfortable. She wonders what she's going to learn between now and then – what more things will she know?

The phone rings as her grandmother's cooking. She brings it through to the girl and the voice that escapes is mid-laughter.

'Hiya, pal!' it says – a new tone from the mumbling of last time.

'Hiya Mum,' she says.

'Here, sorry about the other night. I didn't realise the time.'

The girl tells her it's fine and her mother giggles, telling someone called Broonie to pack it in.

'How's it at your granny's anyway? I bet you're having a great time.'

'Who's Broonie?'

'Just my pal. He's staying over for a bit to help me feel better. And I tell you what, it's working. Feeling loads better, you'll be pleased to hear.'

'When are you coming?' the girl says but the laughter's distant and she's gone unheard.

'Seriously Broonie!' her mother laughs. 'Get lost!'

The girl holds the receiver very tight.

'What was I saying? Aye. Feeling loads better. So how about me and Broonie come and pick you up soon?'

'Alright.'

Mum screeches down the line. 'He keeps... he keeps... He's an absolute riot, you'll love him.'

Smelling dinner in the hallway, the girl swallows a lump.

'You there, sweetie?'

'Aye.'

Her mother sighs. 'What's wrong?'

'Nothing.'

She focuses on keeping her legs out straight in front of her. If she locks her knees and concentrates on that, maybe the wet in her eyes and the lump in her throat will go.

'I can hear it that something's wrong. Christ.' The darkness slips into Mum's voice. 'Very grown up, pal. Very adult. You can never just be happy for me, can you? I'll see you later on.'

She puts the phone back in its cradle. She can just see her – kicking her legs and mixing drinks and taking her time with her hair. She swallows down another lump.

There's nothing else to do with the next day either but muck about in the garden. She isn't bothered about not hanging around with the boys anymore, she's not bothered about Mum. Instead, she counts the steps from one side of the garden to the next. Ten steps. She knows Mum's not coming but when cars pass on the road, she can't help if her stomach pulses.

She finds this beautiful stone beside what used to be the pond. It's small and smooth and pale, the stone – such pale blue. For no reason at all, she bends and snatches it out of the grass and throws it towards the fence. Maybe just to hear the sound of it connecting with the wood, maybe just to watch it bounce. But as the stone leaves her fingertips she's confused by its lightness. She watches it arc across the garden, watches it disappear amongst the sky, watches it reappear and shatter against the fence.

Shatter?

The stone cracks into two and lands lightly on the grass, leaving a dark smear on the wood. Down on the ground the flakes of shell are scattered and between them's something dark, something glossy ...

She looks away. She blushes.

What she saw was primordial and fresh and made her ashamed to have seen it. Something meant to stay hidden, not ready to be revealed. This tiny black bird, wet and bald and jellyish, folded up on itself. It had its legs and wing parts and round bulges where eyes would grow. The inside of its shell was white as plates.

Out of the garden and sitting on the steps, she tells herself if the shell was out of the nest then the baby would've died anyway – they last no time at all without their mother's warmth. She tries to forget it, but she keeps imagining an animal coming in the night to sniff and gnaw at the bird. To carry it around in its mouth. To worry it with claws. She sneaks into the kitchen and finds a container beneath the sink.

She scoops the baby up as best she can and it lies in the bottom of the Tupperware, moving around in its own juices. She covers it with the lid and buries its tiny plastic coffin in the depths of the wheelie bin among bundles of rubbish and hedge trimmings. It's unbearable to have it in there but where else could it go?

A creaking sound behind her. She turns to see her grandad emerging from the shed.

'Hullo,' he says. 'What're you up to?'

She sweats. 'Nothing.'

'Fine. Come and give me a hand.'

He shows her how to secure planks of wood on the shed's entrance so that he can saw them straight. She kneels on the rough timber and her grandad makes piles of short cut-offs. After he's finished, he brings out chicken pieces from inside and they eat them with bare hands, sitting on the old bench behind the shed. The meat leaves her fingers slick and salty; she licks them and gets pieces of sawdust in her teeth. Grandad strips his bones bare of any gristle or cartilage.

'You know,' he says, holding a bone between his fingers to check for anything he's missed, 'you can stay here as long as you like.'

She nods.

'I know what your mum's like better than most,' he says.

This is very warm for her to hear.

He wipes his hands on the knees of his trousers and looks as if he's thinking about something, before making up his mind. 'Right,' he says. 'You wait here a second.'

She waits for a second and then he calls for her to come. Round behind the house, in middle of the back garden, the grass is disturbed and rising from the mound of broken dirt is a wooden birdfeeder. It has sacks of peanuts and fat balls hanging from its perches.

'That's yours,' he tells her. She looks up at the under-side of his face, all chapped skin and folds. She hugs his side and the voice escapes him. 'Easy on.'

Soon, little wheels of finches and sparrows come to land

on the feeder. Grandad's face remains impassive as they appear but his eyes dart around, following their paths. She helps him to sweep up the sawdust from outside the shed. He kneels down with the pan and his knees click. There's a brush in the shed and she uses it on the sawdust to make it into ridges before sweeping it into his pan. They're just about done when he puts the pan down and holds onto his thighs.

'My legs hurt.'

'Are you alright?'

'Aye.' He sucks his mouth and pushes the glasses up his nose. He looks down across all the front gardens and the road, and seems to notice them afresh. 'See that?' he asks, pointing to a spire rising above the rooftops a few streets over.

She nods.

'That's where I got baptised, that's where about I married your gran. See that?' He moves his finger to the right and you can't tell exactly where he's aiming. 'That's the house I grew up in. What's that from here? Two miles – one maybe? What's the church? Half of one, I think.' Smacks his lips. 'That's how it is when you don't stick in.'

His face is solid and dry as wood. She watches its movement.

'I can still mind, down the bottom of the road there, used to be trams. I can mind of them going up and down and clanging and then the council ripped out the lines and made the new road. That all happened and I watched it happen. That's how come you've got to stick in – at the school or wherever.'

They head back towards the house and up the steps and before she closes the door she looks back down the street to see a car coming past. You can't make out the driver until it's already flown by, but it's not going to be Mum. It's never going to be Mum.

In the room at night, she's spoken to. She rubs against the voice of that space, to let herself be angered.

She says, I want to go home. I want my mum.

What? asks the room. Even after that nonsense on the phone earlier?

Yes, she says.

And even after that niceness with the old man?

Yes, she says.

You're a glutton for punishment, it says.

I know, she says, and she's working herself into such a state that sweat's coming through. She's seeing the pair of them on the couch and her mother's arms are around her and she's in so close.

It's not until maybe Tuesday or Wednesday that she hears from the boys. She watches as Darryl's head bounces along, just above the hedge. He rounds the corner and stops when he sees she's there.

'Alright?' he shouts, arcing his arm in a gigantic wave.

She nods, nervous that he'll be angry with her. After all, he was the one who got hit.

'Hiya,' she says.

He bounds up the path and he's got a smear of yellow bruising beneath his eye.

'Come on,' he says. 'You've got to see this.'

'Your eye,' she says.

'What about it?' He's moving from foot to foot, anxious to get going.

'Is it OK?'

'Eh?' he asks. 'What's wrong with it?'

'From ... y'know?'

'Oh that? Aye. Look,' he says and rapidly blinks his damaged eyelid. 'See, totally fine.'

She laughs and gets herself up and he hurries her down the path and into the street. When Darryl runs, his legs kick out to the sides.

THE DOOR HANGS AJAR, ITS TURQUOISE PAINT worn and swords of pale wood showing through. The fuzzy outline of a dreamcatcher rests against its frosted glass. They crouch on the steps below and cast glances behind themselves.

'Whose is it then?' whispers the girl.

Chris leans in. 'Mr Bell,' he says.

'Mr Bell,' says Ally.

'He's this proper weirdo,' says Chris. 'You hardly ever see him. He's huge, massive like, and his arm's all twisted. Like this,' he says and curls his arm in on itself to show her. 'They say folk that've got touched off of his bad arm, their own arm goes all fucked up too.'

She shudders. At home there's a person like that – an albino with a wispy white beard and goggled eyes that if you look into them then your own sweet eyes go goggled too. He lives on the fifth floor and casts fishing lines out the window to the street below that bairns hook empty cans on to.

'We've only seen him a few times,' Darryl tells her. 'Never seen his door open.'

Ally's been glowering at her since she showed up, but he can't resist the gossip. 'When he says huge, he means like *huge* huge.'

Darryl nods. 'My big brother Kev says he's a nonce. Says he'll nonce you as soon as look at you.'

'I wonder where he's got to,' says the girl.

'I wonder how long he'll be,' says Chris.

There's some bickering about who'll go inside and who'll keep watch, but the only fair way to decide is Rock Paper Scissors. Chris draws a Rock to Darryl's Paper and a sweep of relief goes over him.

'If anyone comes,' Chris says. 'I'll whistle.'

Darryl opens the door and slips inside, Ally and the girl behind. A tang of bitterness enters her nostrils as she crosses the threshold. Piled down either side of the hallway are stacks of bound newspapers that leave a narrow path in the middle. You can peer into the kitchen, where all the surfaces are covered in miniature cactuses, connected at the barbs by long trails of cobweb. Most are brown and dry-looking but a couple are recent purchases, more glossy and proud than the rest.

'Weird,' breathes Darryl.

They spend a moment peering around the kitchen and then their eyes meet: on we go.

Above the mantelpiece in the living room is a large, framed paint-by-numbers of a roaring lion and the telly below is still on and the bitter smell's strongest in here, where the atmosphere has a pulse. The girl feels sick at the loneliness of it – the solitary armchair, the drawn curtains, the odour. And even stranger than the painting or the newspapers are the piles and piles of coins. Stacked all around the walls and on the sideboard and fireplace, these neat piles of brown coins.

Darryl picks up one coin from the top of a pile and inspects it. 'What the fuck sort of money's this?' he goes, his voice unbearable in the closeness of the room.

The person in the armchair grunts – the hair tuft seen over the top shakes a little.

'Oh,' says the girl and then Ally's flapping off down the hallway with Darryl following, whistling for help.

The man tries to stand. He's got his good arm grasping and he's sort of lurching upwards and struggling because of his heft. As he hits the ground his body sends out a gust of the smell of the house. She turns and tries to follow the boys but feels a grip at her ankle. He moans up at her, face shiny, the other arm bunched up at his side like a handbag – pale and wrinkled and atrophied.

The girl sprints out, groans and grunts echoing along the walls, and as she emerges into clean air she sees the boys leaping over gardens in three directions.

Gran tries to shush her and calm her down but she's breathless and panicking. 'Slow,' she says. 'Slow. What're you saying about an arm?'

The breath heaving in her chest makes it hard to get the words out. 'House down the street,' she says. 'Big man. Bad arm.'

'Bad arm?' says Gran. 'Are you talking about Alan? Alan Bell?'

She nods.

'Did you say he fell down?'

'Aye, he tipped out his chair and—'

Her gran holds her by the arm and stands up. 'Give me a minute,' she says and rushes from the door, pulling on her big coat as she goes.

The girl's killed him. She's scared him to death and

his heart's burst and he died on the floor, frightened and in pain. His last words, as he rolled and screamed on the floor, were probably lost, probably listened to by coins alone. People died of fright every single day, didn't they? Didn't they? You were more likely to be killed by a horse kick than an airplane crash and people died of fright every day. Young girls are sent to prison every day too – a well-known fact.

Yes, your honour, her mother will say in court, that is my daughter before me. I think it's 100 per cent feasible that she done in that big guy. Like, I once asked her to run to the shop for milk and she scoffed – that's right – scoffed.

That's pure shocking, the jury will interrupt. Your skin crawls just looking at her, doesn't it? Guilty.

The boys all shriek and recoil and pretend they don't want her near them the next day.

'Unclean!' goes Ally. 'Unclean.'

'Here, Stretch,' Chris says, 'your arm's looking smaller.'

She laughs. 'You're a bunch of cowards running off like that.'

'I shat myself,' admits Darryl. 'But what happened – did he get you?'

The girl tells them about Mr Bell toppling from his chair and how Gran had to call the ambulance seeing as how they were friends going way back. How her grandad had remembered when Mr Bell's brother was still living and Grandad used to get drunk with the pair of them in the pub and Mr Bell would flex his little arm to show off for lassies. The story about her own sweet arm withering and atrophying and wrinkling into something like a pale, blind fish was nonsense. She moves her arm in its socket as proof.

Suitably impressed, the boys nod. Ally tells them he saved someone once. Him and a mate from another school that Darryl and Chris wouldn't know snuck into the old carpet factory in Tentshall and his mate had fallen through the floor and had been dangling there until Ally pulled him to safety.

'The press wanted to give me a medal,' says Ally, 'but I turned them down. I was just doing what anyone would've done in the situation.'

'So what happened to him?' asks Chris.

'Blood sugar,' says the girl. 'Too much blood sugar. Or not enough. Anyway, he's in the hospital.'

'I got a cheque for a cool hundred,' says Ally, 'but I just donated it to charity. I just felt like it, that day.'

You can feel the sea before you even see it. The cool breath of it invades your head, chilling your nostrils, salting your lips. They couldn't go back to the treehouse, so they made their way to the beach. It's a long way off, out the estate and through the centre of town and it's this narrow strip of bronze sand but with families playing, with babies marching in the breaking surf. Little diamonds of sun blocked out by swerving kites.

Ally needs help sometimes because of the sand but in general he's alright. The girl runs up to the receding tide, then screeches when she's too slow to back away and its return soaks her trainers.

Once they're bored messing around, they stop at the ice-cream van and put money together so they have enough for cones. There's a low wall at the head of the sand where they sit and eat and Chris laughs as his fringe is blown back and the girl likes the silliness of the white smeared around his mouth.

'We made a fire down here this once,' says Ally.

'Oh,' says Darryl. 'So we did, down at the rocks.'

'Should do that again one time,' says Ally. 'All come down at night and put a fire together and sit round it, or whatever.'

She thinks of her mother. Broonie will go, as the rest. Then she'll appear again, wearing a loose jumper and with her hair all in that messy way and maybe the girl'll be so busy, concentrating so fully on her new life and friends that she'll walk by her and only notice it was Mum after she's gone past and she'll have to glance back over her shoulder and go, Is that you Mum?

And Mum will go, It's me. Can we be together again?

Ally tries to flick some seaweed at her with the end of his crutch but it just sticks to the pole like tape and he has to wash it off in the water and the rest all kill themselves at that.

Then Chris is holding her hand and then he isn't anymore.

The first thing she notices as she enters her grandparents' house is the smell – the smoke of fags. Her beach smile slackens as she stands in the hallway and sees the grey tendrils working over the carpet towards her, as she thinks of her mother grinding fag after fag into ashtrays, walls, saucers. There are voices coming through the closed living room door. The girl goes down the hallway and waits, her hand resting on the handle, wondering how to be.

Except there's a man in there, not her mother. A man sitting at the table with a cigar, his tie undone and his shirt open to the breastbone. Sweat gleams off his collarbones.

'And the thing is,' he's saying, smacking his hands together, cigar clamped in jaw, 'is that they won't learn the bloody language. That's the thing. That's all I'm saying.'

The girl's gran is watching the man with her lips pursed, until she notices the girl in the doorway. 'Hello petal,' she says and ushers her inside. 'I don't know if you'll remember – this is your Aunty Pat and Uncle Bobby.'

The woman sitting beside Gran waves her fingers at the girl. She looks like a hairdresser.

Uncle Bobby leans forward. 'There she is,' he says, holding her by the shoulder. 'The famous niece of mine.' He lets her go, reclamping the cigar within his mad grin and shaking her hand. 'What was I saying?' he asks the room at large.

'Give it a rest, Robert,' says Aunty Pat. 'That's plenty politics for one evening.' She gets up and wiggles her tumbler. 'Who's needing another?'

Uncle Bobby winks at the girl. 'We were just saying, me and your grandad, that me and your Aunty Pat haven't seen you since you were so high.' He shows her how high with his hand. 'It's a damn shame how long we haven't seen you.'

Uncle Bobby accepts his whisky with a warm roar once Pat returns. She dispenses whiskies to the men, gin to the women. The girl gets squash.

'And you're liking the school?' says Uncle Bobby, drinking and wiping his mouth with his palm. 'You're sticking in with all the subjects?'

'Yeah,' she says.

Uncle Bobby nods once, furious. 'That's important,' he says. 'I'm so happy. My boy Neil kept up with his subjects and off he went to college when the time came. Did fuck all with it, mind, but still. Let me ask you a question – how old do you think I am?'

The girl says she doesn't know.

'I am sixty-five years old this month. How about that? Do I look it?'

'No.'

'Did you know I run five miles every morning?'

'Will you leave her alone!' laughs Aunty Pat.

As the evening crawls on the girl keeps to the couch, listening to them gabble about people they knew and the things that happened to them. Outrages and betrayal, none of which mean anything to the girl. Uncle Bobby keeps snapping his fingers and shaking his fist at the girl's grandad, calling him a lucky so-and-so, no matter what her grandad mumbles. He puts the cigar out in a saucer and wipes down his moustache.

He says, 'What a warm feeling it gives me to be here with you all – my brother, his wife and their beautiful granddaughter. How long has it been since we were all in the same room? Such a warm feeling!'

'And I bet that whisky's warm enough and all,' says Aunty Pat.

Uncle Bobby screams a laugh and points at her. 'A sharp woman!' Then, fist on breast, he continues: 'Such a warm feeling. Alec, Margaret. There's only one thing that matters to me, truly, and that's the gift of a good family and all the passion it brings.'

'The gift of the drink,' says Aunty Pat in a stage whisper, to the girl.

Uncle Bobby laughs without sound, wheezing, slapping his knee. 'A sharp woman,' he says, 'right enough. Did I ever tell yous how I met the lovely Pat? Did I tell you? Naw? I was going along in a canal boat and I caught her nudey-sunbathing on the side!'

'That's not funny, Robert,' says Aunty Pat. 'You shouldn't tell lies about me.'

Uncle Bobby's eyes are creased close from amusement. 'They know I'm only doing the mess around, Pat. You *can* meet women on a canal boat though,' he says, suddenly serious. 'Just ask my good friend Fernando, from the taxis – he swears by canal boats.'

The girl can't tell whether her grandad is annoyed or impressed with Uncle Bobby's performance. He lets out little smiles when Bobby roars or is sentimental and sometimes he's looking at the girl and flicking his head towards his brother, cringing.

Uncle Bobby tries to stand but doesn't manage. He leans forward instead. 'Let me propose a toast,' he says. 'A toast to love and to Scotland.'

Her grandad manoeuvres a laugh into a cough. Uncle Bobby undoes another shirt button.

'To love and to Scotland,' he says but the conversation's moving on without him. 'Anyway,' Gran says, leaning forward to peer past Aunty Pat. 'I think it's about time someone got to their bed.'

The girl weaves between the stray tumblers on the carpet and everyone says, 'N'night,' to her.

As she passes Uncle Bobby he reaches out and grabs her shoulder between two fingers, holds her there.

'You mind and look after yourself,' he says. 'Don't end up like your mother.'

In the room, she can't sleep from their noise and she gets to thinking. She's remembering the man that killed girls her own age and slid them into the spaces below trees. The confusion of sleepiness is making it seem like this man was Mr Bell and even though she knows they're different, she's getting scared.

A person gets born, comes out a blank new baby, and grows up into a person that could carry cruelty in their bones and their minds. Not that Mr Bell seemed cruel. But how did a simple gurgling baby grow into a person like that? What happened to a little boy, running to school, hurdling walls, to make them never leave their house for weeks on end and want to close themselves away from anything and not even take their medicine?

Is the secret to cling with desperation to those around you? To forgive them anything – anything at all? Be polite to your mother, never betray your friends, so that when the crack appears there's someone to wipe your chin or give you medicine or tie you to a chair when you wanted to kill?

It's the only solution her mind will give. The boys and Dave Storey – that was a close one. She knows now that if she passes her mother in the road, she's going to grab and hold with every muscle. She's going to make them one again.

She runs out with Gran when they see the ambulance bring Mr Bell home. Her gran tries to give Mr Bell her elbow to help him up the path but he's too vast. He manages himself somehow, teetering along in slippers.

With the windows open, the rooms of Mr Bell's home begin to fill with light and air. Shafts of afternoon sun beam inwards, thick with percolating dust, something like at Mum's house. Gran goes from room to room, deciding how best to begin the big clean. Mr Bell tries to stop her, tries to mime that she needn't bother, but Gran's relentless. She dusts the blinds and the television.

The girl picks up one of the coins from a pile. It is dull and oddly-sided and shows her a young Queen. She pops it into her pocket – just because. Then she finds an empty shoebox and starts to swipe coin piles inside. And then in comes wet, lumbering Mr Bell from the shower. He snatches the shoebox out the girl's hands and water flies from his neck. His eyes are these pennies of anger and the girl backs off, steps away and holds onto the doorframe.

Mr Bell slumps into the armchair, his gown hanging open at the chest. Wet hair parts on the top of his head to show an angry, empty scalp. He holds his bad arm across his belly and looks at the coins that have fallen to the carpet.

Another call comes that night. The ringing doesn't wake her grandparents, so the girl pads out into the hall and answers it herself. The front door's glass is briefly lit by a passing car and thin shadows swing across the floor.

The same wet breath as before. It coughs and makes its tiny damp sounds but says nothing.

'Who is it?' asks the girl.

The voice doesn't hear her, or else wasn't listening because it asks, 'Eh?'

'Who is it?'

'Oh, it's you,' says her mother. 'I thought it'd be your granny.'

'No. They're in bed. It's me.'

'That's nice,' says her mother.

Now's the girl's chance to cement this bond, so that she'll never be left alone, frightened or cold. She thinks of how to say it.

'I'm alright here,' she says. 'I don't mind, I mean, if I have to stay.'

Her mother doesn't respond to that. 'You wanting to get your granny for me, pal?' she asks.

'They're in bed,' says the girl. 'It's late.'

'He's gone,' says her mother.

'Who's gone?' she asks anyway.

'Broonie. Never coming back. And listen, I know I said I'd come the other day but it's not that easy. He took the motor as well. It was his motor, but still.'

The girl remembers the last parent-teacher night up at the school. There was Abbie McMurdo and Lesley Philips and the others and their mums and dads. They were all tucked in and groomed and then there was the girl and her mother and her mother asking Mr Michaels if he was married. You could see one of the other mums hearing and looking over and Mr Michaels coughed.

She remembers her mother nodding when Miss Knight said how good the girl was at art, nodding for so long that Miss Knight said was there was anything her mother wanted to ask?

'Nope,' her mother said. 'You're the boss.'

'It's not about who is or isn't the boss,' Miss Knight said. 'It's about your daughter.'

'We can do He Said She Said until the cows come home,' said her mother.

Abbie McMurdo and Lesley Philips laughed behind their hands when her mother dropped a cup of squash and the orange puddle spread right across the games hall. Her mother did this great big screeching laugh that made everyone turn.

'He's gone away,' says her mother, 'and I'm here, all by myself. That's what happens if no one cares about you, I suppose. If nobody gives a shit. You're just by yourself forever and your own daughter gives you a hard time for it.'

'It's alright,' she tells the phone. 'I said it was alright.'

'Aw,' says her mother. 'Don't play the blame game

with me. At the end of the day, I have to do what's best for the both of us.'

Neither of them speaks then. Her mother's waiting for her to argue, so that she can pretend to be exasperated by the behaviour and put down the phone.

'Listen,' she says eventually. 'I just need to get my head straight, eh? You understand.'

It's not a question. 'I don't mind, Mum,' says the girl. 'So what have you been up to anyway?'

But already she's hung up and there's only dial tone there. She puts the phone down and sees Grandad in the dark at the end of the hall.

'That was your mum,' he says.

The girl nods. 'She sounded weird.'

He takes her through to the kitchen and pours them a glass of water each. The drinking eases the tightness in her throat. Instead of saying anything, she picks at her glass's rim.

Grandad sighs. 'She's a hard woman, our Angie.'

The girl nods.

'There was always something off with her. The single baby I knew that never cried – she laughed. A laugh like a grown human. Babies that young shouldn't laugh. You cried like a good baby. I remember.'

After she fell from the tree at school and got the cast, the doctor had to remove it with a tiny saw. The flesh below was pale and fat and just the feeling of the hospital air moving upon it was like pins and needles.

She can feel that all over now.

THE TREEHOUSE IS STILL OFF LIMITS, so they head for the wasteground to hunt. Darryl has the airgun slung over his shoulders and they're asking her about Mr Alan Bell – was he mental? Did he touch her? What was wrong with him anyway?

'I don't know,' says the girl, enjoying the interest. 'I think he went crazy or something, all them coins and papers, like. You should've seen his house. I went with my gran to help clean up.'

Chris goes goggle-eyed. 'You went *back*?'

'It was minging. I found a mushroom growing down the side of the couch.' She gets only a small knife of guilt from this lie.

'No way,' says Chris. 'An actual *mushroom* mush-room?'

She nods, then remembers. Pats herself down.

'And I took this.'

'Oh, what!' says Darryl. 'That one of them coins?'

'Aye,' she says. 'I just took it.'

They come to a standstill so that Ally can fumble the coin out her grip.

'Did you fuck steal this off him,' he frowns. 'You just found it.'

'I never,' she smiles.

The others hassle the coin from Ally and marvel at it and hold it up to the sun to check for authenticity. It's passed back and forth throughout the journey and then returned to the girl once they reach the wasteground's summit. Darryl kicks up rubble into something like a rest and he kneels with the gun. They take turns on it and it goes off with these hollow pops, straight into a copse of dry bushes.

The girl stands back to watch.

'You have a shot, Stretch,' says Darryl.

They part as Darryl loads it for her and she weighs it in her hands, gets down on one knee. She pulls and a cork goes off in her middle. She fires it twice more, once into empty sky and once into the copse, sending out a fluttering cloud of leaf parts.

'You're a natural,' says Chris.

'She didn't even hit anything,' says Ally.

'You're a natural born killer,' says Darryl.

She hands the gun back and smiles and thinks, What if? What if her pellet flew into the bushes and pierced a bird, a mother bird. Her pellet travelling through wind, then feather, then meat. The bird spinning, trailing pieces of feather and pearls of blood. Dying in the dirt, open eyes, mangled. Babies in the nest – bald and squawking for food.

'I've had enough,' she says. 'Let's go the park.'

And just like that, they follow.

'I used to go shooting a lot with my big cousins,' says

Ally. 'We used to go shooting up at the clay pigeons.'

The girl falls back a touch so that Chris can walk beside her.

'Apparently I've got some of the best aim they've ever seen.'

The wee boy lurks by the park entrance and you can tell he's going to be a pain in the arse before he even opens his mouth. He's got this pudding-bowl haircut and his nose is crusted with snotters.

Ally's slumped down on the other swing, tilting back and forth and not letting Darryl or Chris have a shot. 'What's this clown doing?' he wonders aloud.

Chris and Darryl look over their shoulders and the girl slows her swinging. The wee boy's doing this mad thing where he's pretending to throw a ball into the air and then running towards the swing to catch the imaginary ball. Each throw brings him a few feet closer. Darryl whistles at him to try and get his attention but he either doesn't hear or ignores it. Just keeps flicking his arm into the air and then running with his hands out to catch the falling ball.

'What a mental child,' says Darryl.

In between throwing and catching the ball, the wee boy's wiping his nose on his fat forearm and the girl nearly gags from seeing the slimy trails it leaves on his skin. His bowl cut's shiny and thick and much too clean for the rest of him.

'Watch it,' Chris says.

The wee boy's already right behind him but he throws his hands into the air anyway, wipes his nose on his arm and clatters into Chris's back, falling headfirst into his lap.

Chris shoves him off onto the grass. 'What're you playing at?'

The wee boy pushes the hair off his face. 'Sorry big man,' he says, and his voice is all soft and angelic. 'I never seen you there.'

'Course you did,' Chris snaps. 'I told you to watch it.'

'Aye,' says the wee boy. 'Maybe.'

Ally smacks his crutch against the rubber. 'Never mind your maybes. Get out of here. Get lost.'

'I'll sit where I like,' he tells Ally.

Ally fumes at this. He rubs the crutch between his palms.

'I've never seen you about,' the boy says and it takes the girl a moment to realise he's addressing her specifically.

'We've never seen *you* about,' says Chris.

'Aye you have. I'm always going about here. Never seen you though,' he repeats.

The girl tells him she doesn't stay round here, that she's just there for the holidays. There's something about the boy that makes the girl want to smack him, just because. He reminds her of friends from home and how babyish their playing used to be. She's ashamed of him, of herself.

'That's how come I've never seen you about then,' he says.

Ally's getting impatient. 'Listen,' another rap with the crutch. 'Go on and fuck off, before you regret it.'

The wee boy gives Ally this great big long up and down look. 'And what happens if I don't?'

Darryl can't help but snort.

'What happens? What happens?' says Ally, struggling to his feet. 'I'll show you what happens.'

The wee boy remains impassive. He sniffs a gummy wet sniff.

Ally looks from Darryl to Chris. 'Well?'

Chris stands. 'Let's go,' he says. 'This one's a pain in the arse.'

They get up and trail across the park to the exit, leaving the wee boy down at the swings, cross-legged and watching.

Ally shakes his head. 'Absolute weirdo,' he says and they go out through the hedge-lined pathway and onto the street.

Darryl asks Ally how come he didn't fight him and Ally scowls so hard his forehead goes like knuckles.

'I wish he was here now,' he says. 'If he was here now I'd murder him personally.'

They're at such a loose end that they end up trawling the streets. They get to the bottom of that road and then the girl feels a soft touch on her back. 'Look,' says Chris as she turns. The wee boy's coming down the road after them, trailing his feet and running a stick along the fences, making a soft twanging.

'Go away,' shouts Chris. 'Go on, get.'

The boy keeps coming but he's not looking at any of them. He's watching his feet.

Ally spits. 'This is getting past a joke. If he gets any closer one of you has to do something.'

The boy comes closer. His T-shirt is red and black and blue stripes and the stick's not a stick at all – it's the aerial from a radio or a car. He stops in front of them and looks up. He opens his mouth to speak but before he can get a word out Darryl steps forward and slaps him full across the face.

Everyone shouts. The boy falls down on one knee.

'What?' goes Darryl. 'You said to do something.'

Chris helps the wee boy up as Ally rounds on Darryl. 'I said to do something, aye, but not for you to slap a wee boy.'

'Naw,' says the wee boy. 'That's alright. It's hardly that bad.'

He touches his cheek and shrugs. Nobody knows what to do with him, standing there holding his aerial with a big pink handprint on his chops.

'Are you telling your mum about that?' asks Ally.

The wee boy thinks about it.

'If you tell her, we'll tell her you had your knob out and you were waving it about,' Ally says.

The wee boy shakes his head.

They walk on and he walks with them. You can tell he's pleased because he's bouncing his aerial off the tops of fences rather than dragging it along. 'So,' he says. 'What's the story? What do you lot play?'

'*Play*?' says Ally. 'We don't do any *play*ing.'

'What do yous do then? All I ever see yous doing is hanging about, talking, like a bunch of lassies.'

'We do plenty,' snaps Ally. 'You're probably already in your bed when we get up to most of our stuff.'

'I set my own bedtime,' the wee boy says. 'I was up till two last night.'

'That's ... that's bollocks,' Ally says, clearly rattled.

They come to the end of the road, where you can go up the hill towards her grandparents' and Chris's house. 'Right,' says Chris, pointing downwards. 'On you go. You go that way. We're going up here.'

'It's a free country,' says the wee boy, tapping his bare calf with the aerial.

'Have you no got any pals to go about with?' says Chris.

'I had some,' he admits. 'I was waiting for them outside the wee shop and then they never came out again.'

He follows them up the road, six feet behind. They try to ignore him but there's something awful about him – his lilting voice, his crusted nostrils. That twang, twang, twang that follows him. You can't stop yourself from wanting to hold him down and twist the soft places on him until he squeals.

'Follow me,' says the girl and she leads them all up round the corner and out of the estate, in front of the dual carriageway.

The wee boy's watching from behind. 'That's the big road. That's off limits.'

'*Don't tell us what to do*,' whispers Darryl and they turn and meet a gap in the traffic.

They manage to lose him in the woods, though they're making so much noise he'll be able to find them easily. Coming to a stop in the clearing, they look back the way they've come.

'He's gone,' says the girl.

'What a wee creep,' says Ally. 'He actually gives me the willies.'

'Let's just head up the treehouse,' suggests Darryl. 'I'm fed up of all this walking.'

'What if someone's there?' says Chris.

'And besides,' says Ally. 'We don't want that wee twat knowing where it is.'

'Let's just go,' says the girl and they head back the way they've come.

And the wee boy's hanging off a branch around the corner. He drops to the ground. 'Is it true there's a treehouse up here? A lot of folk say that there is one.'

'Are you like a genius of the woods or something?' asks Darryl and he looks at the rest of them proud, like it's the cleverest thing in the world.

'It's just that I heard that off folk a few times,' the wee boy persists.

'Are you deaf? There's nothing,' says Ally. 'I tell you what, I'm going to lose my temper with this wee bam in a minute.'

The wee boy does this thing where he stands around like he's with them, but he stares at the ground or the trees or over their shoulders like they're strangers in a lift. It makes you want to push him in the face.

'Right! Well, let's get it over with!' explodes Ally and he shambles off into the woods at speed, leading them the few minutes to the treehouse. 'Right,' he shouts. 'There we go. There it is. Happy now? That's it.'

The wee boy actually does the thing where you push your palms into your cheeks to show how shocked you are. 'Wow,' he says, and runs up to the tree. 'It's like off a film or something.'

Darryl, Chris and the girl stand and watch but Ally's so annoyed that he can't stop going back and forward across the clearing on his crutches. 'Yep, it's amazing. And it's spoiled now, so I hope you're pleased with yourself.'

There's a hairy lump on the ground over at the edge of the clearing. The girl goes over and sees it's a dead squirrel, lying rolled up in a ball. She pokes it with her trainer and it doesn't move.

The boys come over too. 'This is a health hazard,' says Ally, and he spins round to shout at the wee boy. 'You. Bring that here.'

The wee boy stands over the squirrel and sizes it up.

'Gimme your thing,' says Ally, gesturing for the aerial. 'What for?'

'I just want to see it.'

'Naw, you'll use it on that,' he points the aerial at the squirrel.

'I won't.'

'Aye you will.'

'Look, just gimme your stick thing and I promise I won't use it on the squirrel. I just want to see how good it is.'

'Honest?'

'Aye, honest.'

The boy hands over the aerial and, despite how annoying he is, it's sad to see him do it because you can tell he values the daft metal stick and he hands it over because he wants them to like him. That's what's disgusting about him – how he shows himself. All those things that the girl's worried about – the boys not liking her or thinking she's slow or pathetic – you can see them written all over the boy. All those things you're not supposed to show.

Ally telescopes the aerial out to its full length and slides it under the squirrel, hoisting it up.

'There,' he says, flicking it off into the undergrowth. 'Was that so bad?'

The end of the aerial's coated in the squirrel's slime. Ally goes to hand it back to the wee boy, slime end first. The boy stretches round to take it by the clean end but Ally moves it so all he can reach is the slimy one.

'Take it then,' he says.

The wee boy tries again to reach past the gunk but Ally won't let him.

'I thought you wanted it,' he says. 'I thought this was the best thing on the whole entire planet?'

The wee boy looks around for help but the rest of them snigger – the girl too. Resigned, he grabs the aerial and it must feel terrible because he drops it and you can see some of the stuff's come off on his hand. This dark greenish smear on his palm, rising to his forearm. They all laugh at that. The same hard, cruel laugh comes out of them all.

'What's the matter?' asks Ally. 'I thought you wanted it?'

The boy crouches down and rubs his hand in the dirt. He tries to do the same with the aerial but he can't get purchase against the ground.

'Let's go up,' says Chris.

The wee boy trails after them and watches as they climb. When they're all up he shouts, 'Can I come too?'

Chris looks down at him. 'If you like.'

The boy goes to get the rope but before he can grab it, Chris pulls it away, out of his reach. More laughter. 'You'll have to be faster than that.'

The boy reaches and the rope gets pulled from him again. They all kill themselves at that.

'Nah,' says Chris. 'Seriously pal, I'm sorry. Go on, take it.'

Once they're bored of that, they let him climb up and once he's up it's as if he's forgotten about the aerial and the rope. Forgotten, because he wants them to like him. The girl shivers, seeing all her own inner workings projected up on the screen of this child.

The wee boy walks around the outside of the treehouse, peering over the edge. 'What do you do up here?' he asks, after he's looked around and sat down.

'Usually we do truth or dare,' Darryl tells the boy.

'Oh right.'

'Aye.' Darryl points to the tree trunk. 'I got off with that last time.'

The wee boy looks at the tree and at Darryl. He scowls and plays with the laces on his trainers.

'Mad, eh?' says Darryl but the boy doesn't look up.

'How about it then?' asks Chris. 'Truth or dare?'

'Well,' says Ally. 'The rule is new folk have to go first. So what is it – truth or dare?'

The wee boy's untied the laces of his trainer and he's wrapping them round his fingers. He looks up and looks right at the girl and he is smaller than she realised.

'Dare,' he says.

Ally must have had it planned because as soon as the boy speaks he picks up one of the beer bottles and shoves it towards him. 'Drink that.'

The wee boy swishes the rainwater around and glances over to the rope, thinking about the excuses he can make that'll get him away. When he takes a sip, he's looking right at her. They all explode when he does it, falling about and laughing and going, 'Aw, what a mink! He did it!'

He's laughing too, wiping his lips.

'What're you laughing at?' asks Chris. 'You're the mink.'

The wee boy laughs again and it sounds so forced. It's just the noise being pushed out – no joy at all.

'You've got to go again,' says Chris. 'It's the rules. You have to go twice.'

'How is that the rules?'

'It's the rules cause it's our game so we say the rules.'

The wee boy says, 'Fine,' and goes back to playing with his lace.

Darryl stands up and clicks his fingers. He bounds across the boards and pulls up his carrier bag. Inside is the air gun and pellets. 'You've got to hold that bottle up and I'll shoot it out your hand.' He feeds a pellet into the gun's barrel.

The wee boy looks like he's going to cry. 'Really?' he asks. 'You being serious?'

'Aye,' say Chris and Ally.

'Those are the rules,' adds Ally.

The wee boy looks over at the rope and stands up. He holds his palm out and balances the bottle on it. His legs are still that chubby way from being so young. Darryl does this mad dog's laugh and wriggles over to the far side of the platform and lies down on his belly. He aims.

All of a sudden the girl sees what's happening: this wee boy's going to get a pellet in his eyes or in his hand. They'll say they're sorry but it'll be too late. They'll have to know they were there when this one child lost his vision or the use of a finger. There's a cold feeling in her hair that might be sweat. It's not the wee boy's fault that he reminds you of the things you're ashamed of.

Darryl wriggles forwards. He clicks the safety off.

If she says something she can stop it but then she'll be on the wee boy's side.

The wee boy jerks his hand up and the bottle goes flying and it chinks down onto the wood and spins, bleeding brown water. For a moment her belly flies – but no, he's OK, scurrying down the rope.

'Aw, he's a chicken,' shouts Darryl and he fires the unused pellet skyward.

'You're all mental,' the boy's voice shouts from beneath the platform.

They go to the side to see him run across the clearing and pick up his aerial. They're all jeering at him and he fires off Vs with both hands, before disappearing into the trees. They sit down again, still laughing about what a weirdo the wee boy was. The girl's laughing as hard as any of the rest.

And then it all trails away and they look down at themselves, only just realising how far that went. They're savage things, thinks the girl. They have savagery inside and all it took was a wee boy to bring it out of them.

Gran says she needs to close her eyes before she can go into the bedroom and she's smiling in that way. The girl complies and listens for the door being opened before inching forwards mummy-fashion, Gran's fingers on her wrist. With eyes closed she can feel those fingers strong and bony and they grip like a bird clenching its claws on a branch.

'Open.'

On the bed's a dress. It's sky blue and it's got these pale cream paisleyish patterns all over and it's grown up. She can't touch it from prettiness.

'Can I?' she says.

Gran laughs. 'Aye, course you can – daft lassie.'

She holds it up against her front and the material's so soft it slides over itself and her body. You can tell it's going to fit in just that right way, like all of Karen's clothes.

'Thanks Gran,' she says.

Gran says she can wear the dress tonight, if she likes.

'No,' she says. 'I want to keep it nice.'

She spends time folding it on the bed, then slips it into one of the room's drawers. As she closes it inside, she sees cars passing on the carriageway ...

It wasn't until they were dashing across the road that she caught the last trace of the wee boy – in two pieces, one in each lane, was his aerial, bent and twisted from tyres.

How can she deserve something so precious after that? How could you dress something as savage as her in something so delicate?

PART TWO

THE AUTOMATIC DOORS OPEN AND LET out a burst of that chemical smell. They get changed in separate rooms and when Grandad comes out you see his chest is thick with grey wire and his nipples hang like little bags. Back home, when her mother takes her to the pool, she sits in the stalls because the pool water's bad for her hair, but Grandad does lengths and the girl sees how long she can be under water for. Through goggles there's all the fleshy kicking legs and stomachs. It's pure quiet down there, with the screech of bombing bairns and lifeguard whistles only reappearing when she breaks the surface again.

That must be like dying or getting born. You're out there somewhere, watching all humans walk or fight or kiss and there's something between you and it's not till you pierce the material that you can hear them and see them properly. Then you die and you go back under and it's quiet and close.

There's one great big diving board at the pool, a

mile high. Just the biggest and the maddest go up there. The girl floats in the shallow end, her mouth below the waterline, breathing like a crocodile, watching the ones brave enough to dive from that height. Beside her in the shallow end are the bobbing families: bairns fighting with floats and mums holding up babies so they can get their legs used to kicking. It's making her warm, all the hot bleached air rising to meet her.

She spots a group of girls near the lowest board, holding onto the side and watching divers. Could be the girl's age, maybe a touch older. They're all there together. Then there's a boy climbing the ladder to the top board. He looks a bit like Chris. Same dark hair, same hard brown arms. He pauses and uses a breath. Someone in the pool cheers for him and he walks along the board. He bounces on the end a few times and all the screaming and the noise from the water vanishes.

A crack.

He's falling over himself and spinning and straightening out and you can feel something move. He breaks the surface and goes along beneath it and then the girls are laughing again and someone gets whistled for bombing. She loses him in the muddled underwater. She reaches for the side and puts her hand on a plaster that's clinging to the tiles.

They drink their after-swim slushes as they walk through the caravan park. The girl's eyes sting and lips tingle from the chlorine and she can feel sugar and E numbers course through her from the slush. She can feel the ice melt in her belly.

Grandad takes a sip from his. His face screws up. 'Christ,' he says. 'What sort of garbage is that?'

They split up on the way back to Uncle Bobby's caravan

– the girl wants to walk via the beach. There's sun shining on the water and making lines of shimmering whiteness between horizon and girl. She makes her way through the red-skinned families, shouting, burning barbecues, and walks into the sea barefoot, to find the water warm. Out in the emptiness of the sea she places a camera on a buoy. It wobbles and droplets collect on the screen, but you see the girl on the shore.

Alone. Perfect.

The family in the caravan next to them have a stereo turned all the way up. The dad keeps thumping his boy on the back of the head and the boy with the thumped head plays swingball against himself for hour after hour. As she passes, he pokes his pinkie finger out of the zip in his shorts, like a little wriggling knob.

Gran and Grandad are playing cards on the patio.

'Go for a fish,' says Gran.

'You're just meant to say go fish,' Grandad replies.

Her gran says that it's all too complicated and smiles at the girl. 'What do you think then?'

'It's lovely, Gran,' says the girl.

Gran's eyes crease from pleasure.

Swimming makes her need, so she heads inside, into the cramped toilet. As she's going, the girl picks up one of the magazines to read for a minute, but something slips out and flutters to the floor. It's a Polaroid photo of Aunty Pat and she's doing this pose that shows off her bare privates – these sprawling red hairs! – and the belly folds above all slip amongst themselves. In a panic, the girl tries to flush it away but the card jams in the toilet's opening and gets stained a little blue by the chemicals. Holding her breath, she fishes it out and doesn't breathe until the photo's rinsed in the sink and wrapped up in toilet paper in her back pocket.

Bobby and Pat arrive back from their day trip after tea. They've been caught in the rain someplace and Uncle Bobby's moustache is slick. The girl can't look at Aunty Pat, her make-up all smudged and towelling herself off in the living area – she's so paranoid that even Bobby's watching her from the corner of his eye.

'Alec? Do you mind DiFranco's?' he asks.

'Aye,' Grandad says, leaning on a worktop in the caravan's tiny kitchen. 'Course I do.'

'We stopped off there today.'

'Is that right?'

'Aye. Guess what it is now?'

'No idea.'

'A bloody Boots-the-Chemists! This country!' he marvels. 'I mind when me and auld Alec over there would get the bus down from town so we could sit there in DiFranco's like a pair of plums,' he winks at the girl, 'all so's that your grandad could get the chance to *not* chat up your grandma.'

Grandad gets this reddish blush in the creases round his mouth.

'Aye,' says Bobby. 'She was some woman in her day, right enough.'

Aunty Pat makes a groaning sound as she wedges herself into the toilet to change her tights. 'Eugh,' she says. 'What an old letch.'

'DiFranco's,' says Uncle Bobby. 'Feels like a lifetime ago.'

Gran tells the girl how she'd served Grandad ham and chips for forever and then this once he'd reached out and

122

held onto her hand. The girl gets a great wooziness from hearing that. She can see the two of them in their distant past, in their black-and-white youngness. She sees this boy of her grandad and he has the same nerves as any person might have.

The caravan shakes a little from wind and they all look up.

'Looks like we've brought it with us,' says Aunty Pat and they rush to the windows to see sheets of rain wash down the glass. A great heavy summer storm, with the fuming clouds rolling in from the ocean and the air tasting like salt and something tangy. People shout and run across the park, sunburnt families roar and corral wriggling bairns with rolled up windbreaks and kites.

'Watch this,' says Uncle Bobby, rummaging in the carriers they brought back. He stands with one hand behind his back, the other he uses to make a cone round his mouth. He voices a trumpet, then says, 'Ladies and gentlemen, I present to you, the esteemed Double Lion Blend,' and sweeps the bottle of whisky from behind his back.

He shows it off to everyone and the girl's belly does a flip. There's something about adults and drink … When they get into those sweating moods from it, when they want to corner you in a kitchen and tell you what a nice girl you've grown into. How you remind them of them at your age.

Out the main window she sees that the thumped boy's back, swingballing topless in the artificial light, in the rain.

When the dark comes, the weather trails off into mist. Lights are on in the caravans and you can see the families inside. They look happy, like on adverts. One family looks like they're even doing a jigsaw together. Down

123

on the beach there's a fire and some older kids are doing screaming. Uncle Bobby keeps filling everyone's tumbler without asking and the telly's blaring. He keeps saying they should all go on holiday together, but a proper one – Spain or that.

'Anyway. Enough about us old bastards,' he says, turning on the girl. 'What's *your* story?'

The girl holds onto the elbow of her other arm.

He laughs at her. 'Like, what is it you get up to at your age?'

'Just this and that,' she says.

'*Just this and that*. In my day – listen – in my day we used to pick tatties, potatoes. Did you know that? With our bare hands I mean, not with your machineries or your combine harvesters. Christ no. Howking it was called. Every morning in the October holidays the farmer picks us up and we spend the day pulling tattie after tattie in his field.'

Grandad nods. 'It was terrible,' he says.

'It was alright money though, wasn't it Alec? Five bob maybe? Oh my Christ was it hard though. I used to think my back would break. But there's nothing like that now. It was good for us all that. Listen: do you get to choose your subjects up at the school yet?'

'No,' says the girl. 'I'm starting the high school after the holidays.'

'Ah Christ,' he goes. 'They mollycoddle them these days. You're not meant to say that, not these days, but they do. Did you know I left the school when I was fourteen? How about that, eh? Fourteen? Anyway. What's the plan for after – after school, like?'

'Leave her alone,' says Aunty Pat. 'She's only young yet.'

'Aye,' he says. 'You think I'm unaware? But you've got

124

to have a plan, do you not? Women like this,' he says, pointing at Aunty Pat, 'think they can just sink their teeth into the first chap with a trade that comes along. But it's not like that these days.'

'I maybe wouldn't mind being a vet,' says the girl.

Uncle Bobby dismisses the idea with a wave of the hand. 'And what about the lads? What's your boyfriend called?'

'Come on,' says Gran. 'Look at her.'

The girl feels the condensation of the caravan – to run out and breathe the cold air would be heaven itself.

Uncle Bobby holds his glass in the air. 'What? Can I not ask a simple question? Is Uncle Bobby too uncouth for you and yours?'

'That isn't how it is,' says Gran.

The girl looks at Grandad. He holds his tumbler between his thighs and his eyes are inside it.

'Cookie-bun!' says Uncle Bobby. 'I'm only asking the lassie simple questions about the school and boyfriends and so on. She knows I'm just being daft, doesn't she?'

The girl sort of nods.

'Say it then,' says Uncle Bobby. 'Say to me I'm just being daft.'

The air leaves a sheen on the girl's face as she slips out and it sparkles down the corridor of caravan lights.

'Here,' says the thumped boy. 'Wanting a game?'

They play on the swingball and the girl's facing the caravan and she can see Bobby standing up and gesturing and she can't tell if he's shouting or laughing.

'That your dad?' asks the boy. 'He looks like an absolute rocket.'

'My uncle. I've only just met him.'

The boy nods and serves. 'My dad's a rocket,' he says.

'Aye,' she agrees. 'I seen him,' sending the swingball back. 'He's always thumping your head.'

The boy nods, scowls. 'I'm gonnae burn down this whole world one of these days.'

The beach is empty. Something must have scared off the teenagers and their fire. She manages to throw the Polaroid at a good angle but the tide brings it back and deposits Aunty Pat and her privates at the girl's feet. She tries again and it lands out on the water far enough away that once the waves take it, they move it out to sea. A perfect square of white reflected moonlight, drifting.

The next night, at the disco, Uncle Bobby and Aunty Pat are dancing themselves sweaty among a crowd of children. The girl sits in the corner with her grandad – two old souls, watching the crowds.

One quick count is all it takes to ask it: one, two, three.

'Do you like Uncle Bobby, Grandad?'

He chuckles, wrinkling his brow across the music.

'When Uncle Bobby's talking, you get this face.'

'You're sharp as a tack,' he says, moving his glass across the table.

The disco lights make the ice cubes green, then red.

'See, the thing is, when someone's your brother or sister you get so close. How do I say it? It's like, I always know what your Uncle Bobby's going to say before he says it.'

The girl's seen brothers and sisters not getting along from films and telly. A book she read had a girl that was so jealous she killed her sister.

'There's also... Christ, sorry. There was this other thing, years and years ago. Someone said something about Bobby that ended up not being true. How do I say this? Someone told your granny and me something about your uncle Bobby, and we asked him about it. He didn't take it well.'

'So he's annoyed at you?'

'He was at war with me since he was born – even when I wasn't at war with him.'

Maybe it was a murder or something, whatever Uncle Bobby was accused of? Maybe someone said, we saw your Bobby and he was there at the murder scene, or even doing the murdering. She wouldn't put it past him. He was the type to be at a murder scene, setting the record straight. Grandad brings the glass up to his face and he's obscured by the green, red, green fluid.

People did tell lies though. For example, she remembers her mother saying Grandad hit her, all the time.

The thumping man and his family are at the next table and on stage a performer's doing hypnotism and puppeting this wee dummy.

'Great show!' shouts the man, his neck as red as soup. 'What's he going to come out with next? I'm fucked if I know!'

Uncle Bobby appears now that the dancing's over. 'Hey you,' he says. 'Less of the language if you please.'

The man's clapping and wiping away tears at the hypnotist pulling a stream of hankies from the dummy's mouth. Uncle Bobby's still bristling but Gran says for him to get a round in.

'OK, but I'll need a hand,' he says and hoists the girl up by the shoulder so that she can weave with him through the club's darkness to the bar. He nods at folk as they pass and he walks in this way – arms wide-out and his bones moving with oil. They wait for the round and the girl looks at the upside-down bottles behind.

'You're enjoying yourself?' he asks.

'Aye,' she says.

'Good,' he says, nods at the crowd. 'Plenty boys here for a lassie your age, you know? See anything you like?'

Something clenches and she finds she cannot move, cannot respond.

'What about the boyfriends?' he says. 'Don't be shy. You can tell me that sort of stuff.'

She does something with her mouth. His eyes have a greasy sheen to them. She can picture them looking through a camera's innards, using up the things that they capture. What if he notices the photo's gone from the caravan toilet?

'Come on,' he says. 'There must be lads sniffing round you already. You think I don't know how it is? You think I don't know what it's like to be young?'

Two of the glasses go down on the bar and Uncle Bobby fishes in his jeans for cash. The girl floats upwards to the lights and lost balloons.

As he's fishing, he winks at her. 'You think I don't know what *your* sort gets up to?'

They're walking home and Uncle Bobby starts singing and puts his arms around her grandparents.

'Speed bonnie boat,' he sings, 'like a bird on a wing. Onward, the sailors cry!'

'Will you shut your pus?' someone says from behind, and it's the thumping man, stumbling through the club door.

'Is he trying to play the big man?' Uncle Bobby asks of no one.

The thumping man points at Uncle Bobby's face. 'You need to show some respect. Some folk's bairns are in bed.'

The swingball boy and his brothers are doing kung fu behind glass in the club's vestibule.

'He *is* trying to play the big man,' Uncle Bobby says and takes off his sovereign ring.

'I think the pair of yous are disgusting,' goes the thumping man's wife.

Aunty Pat cocks her head. 'And who asked you?'

Then the wife is screaming because Uncle Bobby's barrelled into the man's stomach. He has him by the neck on the ground, right under the lights and the swingball boys are up against the window and are banging on it and crying. Grandad tries to pull his brother away but ends up falling backwards with his legs in the air and Bobby's clocking the man and the man's slapping Bobby until he's on the floor too and they have their heads trapped in each other's elbows.

The big light shows them orange and wet on their faces and saying words the girl doesn't know.

Gran's crying for Bobby to stop it, to let him go.

'Is he the big man now?' asks Uncle Bobby, speaking into the thumping man's armpit.

'I never even said I was the big man!'

'Maybe not, but you were acting it sure enough.'

The manager and a barman run out and try to get them under control but they can't work out who's at fault. Uncle Bobby claims the thumping man called him a wog, which just makes no sense and confuses everyone.

'I never realised it was an illegal offence to protect your family,' says Uncle Bobby, wriggling under the manager's grip.

'We're just trying to find out what's happened,' says the manager.

The barman brings the thumping man up into a kneel and says, 'Can we just agree that we've all had a bit much to drink, a bit too much sun, and forget about it?'

'He's a bloody animal,' says the thumping man's wife and you don't know which one she means.

'I'm not agreeing to nothing,' says the thumping man. 'I know my rights and I'm being detained against my will.'

'Says the one throwing out racialisms so all and sundry of the park can hear,' says Bobby.

'Says the one breaching the peace,' says the thumping man.

And then they both get free and go at each other and a jet of blood from the man's mouth lands on the side of the vestibule, and the swingball boy sees it fly. He sort of runs to the glass and watches his father and it's obvious then that the holiday is over.

Her grandparents' street opens up like a flower as they turn into it, as the afternoon's coming to a close. Only a handful of cars are parked and the sky's like pool water. They go past Mr Bell's house and Chris's house and her gran goes, 'Oh my God,' when she sees their front door is sitting open.

Parking and unbuckling his belt, Grandad's up the path like a shot. Gran reaches back and squeezes the girl's knee and they wait until he comes out again, rubbing his cheeks and disappearing around the side.

And then, opening the front door and squinting at the sun, shading her eyes and making the dolphin tattoo on her shoulder ripple, is her mother.

Gran's breath catches in her throat.

EVERYONE IN THE KITCHEN THINKS IT'S their job to make the tea. The girl's mother gets out mugs and so does Gran: eight mugs total. Both grandparents try and fill the kettle – boiling and clouding and rumbling over the conversation.

'Why would you not say if you were taking her on holiday?' her mother asks.

Drawers slamming, cupboard doors opening and closing.

'But Angie,' says Gran. 'You never said you were coming back for her.'

Her grandad's wiping the worktop, looking in the cupboard for the sugar that's already on the table. The girl watches from the doorway, all of them squeezing past each other in the steam and talking to each other without meeting eyes.

Four mugs land on the tiny table in the living room.

'Which one's the one with sugar?' says Grandad.

'It's looking a bit tired in here,' says her mother.

'It's the blue mug that's yours, Alec,' says Gran.

Someone hands the girl a mug and she squeezes between her mother and Gran on the couch, Grandad opposite.

She counts.

Everyone looks into the circle of tea below them.

'Anyway,' says Gran. 'You shouldn't have fallen asleep with the front door open like that. Anyone could've waltzed in.'

Her mother slips the girl a wee sideways look, like they're on the same team. She's a famous person and the girl can't look away.

'As if they've got anything worth stealing, eh?'

'Angie,' says Gran. 'It's just safety, isn't it?'

'What?' snaps her mother. 'And is it safety to take the bairn away to – I don't even know where! – without letting her own mother know about it?'

Grandad tips his mug, making a face like he's taking medicine.

'Oh hell,' says Gran. 'It's not worth falling out over, is it?'

'No,' says her mother.

Gran works the folds out of her skirt. 'So. How are you doing? You're feeling better I take it?'

The girl's mother puts her mug down and flexes her bicep to show them how much better she's feeling. 'Back to full strength,' she winks at the girl.

Gran sniffs. 'OK then.'

She remembers how she dreamt it: her mother returning contrite, climbing her grandparents' stairs on hands and knees. Now here she is, winking and flexing like nothing's happened, and here's the girl, watching her and forgiving her everything.

132

The girl's mother leans back and gulps some tea. 'So how was it then, the holiday?'

Her grandparents give the girl a look, so she goes, 'Fine. We went swimming.'

'Swimming? Very nice.'

Grandad stands. 'Go and play in your room for a bit,' he tells her.

Play in her room? When has he ever seen her *play*? How old does he think she is? This is the whole problem with adults who are not her mother – they don't understand what she is.

All she can hear is mumbling through the bedroom door, even with her ear pressed right up against it.

What happens now? she asks.

The room exhales. You go home?

The girl tries lying on the floor with her ear by the crack at the bottom. I hope so, she says.

And then what? asks the room.

And then we're back to normal.

The room laughs.

Her mother wakes her up by stroking her painted nails over the girl's cheeks and lips.

'Hi there, baby,' she says.

She's lying beside her on the bed, fully clothed. The room's in darkness.

'Hello,' says the girl.

Her mother climbs over her and envelops the girl in arms and legs. Her nose pokes into the nape of the girl's neck.

'Ah,' says her mother. 'I've missed this.'

Nuzzling deeper, the girl lets Mum's arm fall across her face.

'Me too,' she says.

They lie like that for a while. The girl keeps as still as she's able to stop it from breaking. The breath on her neck is deep and warm and she can feel it collect in her hair.

After a bit, Mum whispers, 'Are you awake?'

'Yes.'

'I'm sorry I let you go.'

The girl smiles to herself in the darkness. 'That's alright,' she whispers back.

And in her dream she's within a cave: water dripping, coldness. She walks over little streams in the rock, in the gloom, following the sound of water roaring. In the puddles that form there are the pale flashes of fish and her bare toes tickle their surfaces as she steps from stone to stone. At a bend in the path she leans against the cave wall and is surprised to find it soft. It warms her back and she wakes bundled in arms.

Mum's making instant coffee, filling the kitchen with the static of her movements, her hair matted and sticking up at the back like brambles.

'Where do they keep the effing sweetener?' she says, pacing and throwing open cabinets.

'We don't usually have the telly on during the day,' her gran says when Mum puts it on.

'Well I'm on my holidays, technically,' says Mum and she puts her feet up on the coffee table. 'Where's Dad? Is he not wanting to spend some quality time with his best daughter?'

'He's out working in the shed.'

'Oh aye,' smiles Mum. 'His shed.'

The three of them watch the adverts and a man tells

them they could be owed millions of pounds in compensation. The girl's mother says she should claim for her bad back from working nights down the pub.

'Them beer barrels,' she says.

It seems nothing's changed in a lifetime round here because Mum knows the neighbourhood like the back of her hand. She points to houses to show the girl where her friends used to stay. There's a bridge going over the railway line. Squatting down, she checks the graffiti, but it's all new.

'This is where my pals and I used to come to have a fag when we couldn't face the school.'

'When you were my age?' the girl asks.

'Aye, maybe. Maybe a bit older.'

They keep wandering, and the girl keeps starting to count, wanting to ask her mother: what happens next? But before she can get any momentum going, Mum will start to tell her that someplace used to be a decent pub back in the day or that a building's new because the old one burnt down. They stop at the post office and Mum buys them a penny mix and it's all the best ones, eggs and turtles, and they share it out as they walk.

'I suppose you've been having a great time up here,' Mum says as she tears apart a fried egg.

'It's been OK.'

'Just OK?'

'Aye. OK.'

'I thought maybe you wouldn't be pleased to see me. I thought you'd be having too much of a carry on up here.'

The girl tells her about the boys and what they've been getting up to and Mum pokes her in the ribs.

'You well fancy that Chris boy,' she says.

The girl burns.

'I can tell from the way you're talking. We've got a lot of catching up to do.'

When she says things like that it's like the girl's head's full of warm water. She asks Mum how it's been at home.

'At home?' Mum says, taking the girl's hand and swinging it. 'At home's been ... For a bit I was in one of my sad moods and I wasn't sleeping right and I couldn't get my head together. Then I was in one of my laughy moods and that was when Broonie came round and he was staying there for a bit but I said to him he needed to get going since my special wee champion was coming home soon.'

The girl laughs.

'I'll maybe need your help getting the place sorted when we get back though. It's maybe a bit messy but nothing two strong lassies like us can't sort out.'

'That's fine,' says the girl.

'We could have our own little party once we're back. Like we could get chips and salsa from the big Tesco's and maybe a new film or that? How does that sound?'

'Aye,' says the girl. 'Great.'

'We'll stick about here for a day or two, see the sights, relax, then we'll hit the road. Just the pair of us together again, eh? Just the pair of us together?'

The girl can't even reply.

They take the bus into town and Mum asks the barmaid if the girl can come in for food. The barmaid says it's fine so they get themselves a table by the windows.

The girl picks up her cola and Mum gulps her wine. 'Ah,' she says, and then, 'so.'

'So,' says the girl.

'Tell me about your holiday! Where did you even get to?'

She opens her mouth to answer but before she can get a word out there's a man looming over them.

'Is that you?' he asks Mum. 'Angie?'

Mum leaps into the air to throw her hands around the man. 'Stig!' she says. 'Christ man, it's been ages.'

'I know, I know,' he says into her hair. 'How've you been, love?'

They break apart and stay looking at each other. 'Not bad. Not so bad.'

He smiles and nods and clocks the girl. 'I'm Stig,' he says, pointing to his head. 'Like *of the Dump*.'

'Me and Stig go way back,' Mum tells her. 'We were at the school together.'

They're standing up and talking about people the girl doesn't know so she drinks her cola through the lemon for added flavour. Stig's not like the other men she's seen her with. He's broad and his smile's daft and he has all that hair and beard. He flicks his head towards the table in the corner and asks if they want a game of pool.

Mum twiddles with the top of the girl's head. 'Sorry,' she says. 'This is a girls' day out. No boys allowed.'

It's way into the evening before they leave. Mum gets drunker and drunker, buying herself wines and the girl colas, and the girl doesn't even mind. She'll listen to her mother's stories all night if she'll let her. Then when it's time to go, Mum kisses Stig on the mouth as he's saying goodbye and the whole pub cheers for them.

'Let's get out of here before I make a fool of myself,' she whispers to the girl, like they're friends.

They get a taxi up the road and halfway home Mum realises she's got no money for the fare. The driver calls them arseholes and they're kicked out by the harbour, so they peg it to the water and sit down on the dock and let legs dangle over the side. Nothing breaks the surface and a parade of gulls sleep on the sea wall. Mum spits into the water and sighs, extra extra beautiful under the moon.

'Shall we just jump ourselves in and have done with it?' she asks and takes the girl's hand. 'Just jump in,' Mum says to the water. 'Plop.'

The harbour's illuminated from behind and shadows fleet over the sea wall, huge and lonely.

Mum laughs. 'Look at her face!'

She stands them up and they go walking, out over town. They slip through a garden and over a fence. Across some bare fields they creep as the stars go on and on and the cold moon hides and reappears from behind black clouds. Foxes fight or mate nearby and yowl like naughty babies. The girl falls behind as they pick their way over tractor tracks in the dirt, baked into sharp canyons, following the footprints Mum leaves her. Far off to the east you can see the smear of trees where the treehouse is and the girl puts up her hood as bats or swallows flit past in low clouds. Together, they climb up onto a dirty hay bale, not caring how it gets their hands and arses black.

Wind touches and they hold hands. They stay out and watch the sky. Nothing's ever been so warm.

Next day Mum sleeps in, her dreaming breath boozy in their shared bed – the girl lying beside her, not moving, feeling her presence.

First thing, Mum checks the mobile. Stig's been in touch and he's coming to pick up Mum in half an hour and does the girl want to come out driving?

Her legs take on this soreness and she holds them out

tight beneath the sheet. She says she doesn't want to go but it's fine if Mum does.

When they've gone, her gran corners her in the kitchen, asking the girl if she knows how much drink Mum had the night before.

'Don't know,' the girl says, knowing exactly how much.

Gran nods once and walks away.

She gets the boys loitering on the street. 'Alright Stretch?' they say.

'How was the caravan?' asks Darryl.

She says it was fine and tells them she's been busy since Mum's taken time out of her hectic schedule to come and see her.

'We're thinking about putting our money together to buy a rat,' says Ally.

'It would be like a mascot,' says Darryl.

'They're selling them down at the shop,' says Ally.

The girl nods. 'Alright,' she says, showing she's not keen on the plan.

'I said it was a daft idea,' says Chris.

'No you never,' says Ally.

'A pet's a big decision,' agrees Darryl.

'My mum and dad,' says Chris, 'were saying about maybe Portugal this year for our holidays.'

'I went to Portugal,' says Ally. 'I got totally pished every night.'

'When did you go to Portugal?' demands Chris.

'When I was ten, obviously.'

'You went to Butlins when you were ten, didn't you? And how could you get pished every night if you were only ten?'

Ally says that he can't remember whether or not it was

Butlins, but that even wee babies have a glass of wine with their tea, at Butlins.

'It's a different culture down there,' he says, then, 'Oh shite I meant to say—' He starts rummaging in his bag, struggling with the crutches, digging in the depths. He winces from the effort of it.

'If it's another porno, I'm not interested,' says Chris.

'You wait,' says Ally.

The boys both go, 'Woah,' when Ally slides a bottle out his rucksack, showing it off like a salesman. It's a sort of booze called BuzzBottle and it's coloured blue like mouthwash.

'Where did you get it?' says Chris.

'One of my other mates can get served down the newsagent's,' says Ally.

Chris is hesitant. 'Where would we even drink it?' he asks. 'We can't at my bit.'

'Wherever,' goes Ally. 'Down the beach.' He looks around. 'What about you Stretch? You in?'

'Aye,' she says. 'Could do.'

'Who're these other mates?' asks Chris. 'Since when have you got other mates?'

Ally smiles. 'There's a lot I get up to you know nothing about.'

'So when are we doing it?' asks Darryl.

'We could go down the beach after tea on Thursday,' says Ally and they all agree – Thursday it is.

Later in the day, this big lad turns up and he's the spitting image of Darryl. His neck is long and his ears and lips protrude from his miniscule head. It's Darryl's big brother, Kev.

'Right,' he says. 'Shall we get on with it?'

'Right,' says Darryl and they all stand and follow Kev.

The girl walks beside Chris and she asks him what's going on.

'He's going to get Dave Storey,' says Chris. 'He showed up again when you were away and kicked Darryl in the throat.'

Ally clangs his crutches off of lampposts and bins as they walk. 'This'll be amazing,' he says. 'We're going to end him.'

They stop outside a house with car parts laid out on the grass. Kev climbs up on the fence and swings back and forth to make the posts rattle. Dave Storey's big head appears at one of the top windows. He's serene up there, looking down at them.

When they fight, Kev falls over and hurts his hip on one of the engine parts. Storey tries to climb on top but Kev slips away and brings his hand down on Storey's head. They fight until Storey's bottoms slip down and you can see his arse and thighs and they're all white and hairless and fat. Kev gets on top of Storey's chest and slaps at his face and makes him eat grass. The girl's remembering Uncle Bobby and the thumping man and because of that she's remembering Uncle Bobby at the bar.

She feels herself floating again.

Storey's hopping mad, face red and spitting. They leave him pulling up his bottoms, lying on his back.

'Keep your hands off of my brother,' says Kev without looking back.

He leaves them back near home and he gives Darryl a quick, strong hug, saying to let him know if there's any more trouble. They watch him skulk off and their faces are lit like bulbs.

Mum goes out with Stig again next day. As she rushes down the hallway to the sound of him peeping his horn, Gran tries to intercept her.

'Angie,' she says. 'What's going on?'

Mum tries to get past. 'Eh? What you on about?'

'Where are you going?'

'Just out!'

'It's not fair on the bairn. She needs to know what she's doing.'

'She doesn't mind,' says Mum. 'I asked her.'

Gran throws wide her arms. 'But she's hardly going to tell you.'

'Here, pal,' says Mum, getting the girl in from the kitchen. 'Do you mind if I go out for an hour or two with my mate?'

They're both looking down on her – both asking her something unsaid.

'No,' says the girl. 'I don't mind.'

The front door opens and closes and her gran stands for a second beside the hanging spider plant, brushing something off her cardigan sleeve.

You can smell the difference already. The newspapers are still there but they've been dusted and all the cobwebs have been cleared from the cactuses in the kitchen and the withered ones are gone. Her gran makes cups of tea in the kitchen and the girl goes with Mr Bell. They don't talk or look at each other. He grunts as he moves himself down the chair. The girl thinks of the stolen coin – back home, beneath her mattress, within the pages of the magazine.

Mr Bell shows the girl the videos he has stacked up near the telly. She splits them into three smaller piles and shows Mr Bell each one – if he wants to keep it, he gives her a thumbs up. The rest her gran'll take down the charity shop. Mr Bell slumps in his chair with this look showing humiliation, hating to rely on a wee lassie for these most basic tasks.

Halfway down the second batch she finds this video with a woman on the front showing off her privates, like Aunty Pat. The plastic's slippery in her hands straight away and she catches Mr Bell's eye. His neck hangs in a chunk around the jowl – he touches his little arm with the other, across the belly.

'Do you want it or not?' she asks.

He nods and gives this wincing smile and the girl throws the video down. She looks around for a while, hands on thighs. She's seeing Uncle Bobby rummage in his jeans for change, seeing his winking smiling face lit up under the dancing lights.

She stands up.

'My mum's come to get me,' she says. 'I probably won't have to come down here ever again.' She listens for her grandmother and traces a finger down a pile of coins on the sideboard. 'I can't believe you've kept these for so long – you're a creep.' She looks him right in the eye, and he does what a dog does when you look it right in the eye.

With the gentlest flick of her finger, she tips the pile over and it brings down several more and they cascade onto the carpet with a brittle rattle. It's her mother's finger she's using.

Mr Bell's eyes bulge.

She flicks off another pile, then a third.

Mr Bell watches the coins fall and he blinks. She wills him to do something, but you can tell from how he ogles the falling coins that he's scared. She can feel what he's frightened of, and it's her.

There's savagery in her blood, just like her mother.

His shoulders move like hiccups and his neck and

eyelids are wet and red. He opens his mouth for breath.

She says, 'What's the matter?'

Mr Bell shakes his head. His little arm wriggles as the body spasms.

'Tell me what's wrong,' says the girl.

A deep inhalation. 'Brother,' he says.

Only then does she recall what her gran said about the newspapers in the hallway – this man's brother died. Her grandad knew the pair of them.

Brother, he tells her. Lightning, he tells her. Walking home from the pub in a storm – cats and dogs. Old fashioned umbrella – iron spokes. *Voom*. He flew and landed on cobblestones. Umbrella like a bent and twisted crow. These ropes of grief lash out from Mr Bell and hold the girl and she feels all of it – feels the crack and sulphur and white electric fire. Feels the road rattle the ambulance as it bumps along.

She leans back on her heels and watches Mr Bell.

You could hold on as hard as you wanted to a person. You could grip until your nails drew blood. You could forgive them anything and still nature might send down its living electricity and *Voom* – that would be it.

She can see this bird flying across the sea with the land below it coming and going beneath the waves.

Stig takes the pair of them bowling one night and her gran says it's OK as long as they're back for tea. Mum insists on raised bumpers and she throws the ball with two hands, twirling round her toes once she's struck, beaming to the girl – only to her. The girl comes second, after Stig, and he buys milkshakes from the counter.

He drops them off afterwards and they go up the path to the house hand in hand.

'He's alright isn't he?' Mum asks and the girl can be honest when she answers – yes.

Her grandparents are waiting at the kitchen table.

'Jesus,' says Mum. 'What're you doing sitting in the dark like that?'

'It's your tea,' says her gran. 'We said, didn't we?'

So they have to eat together and the girl's so full of strawberry and chocolate that she struggles with the lamb, which is coolish and congealing. She watches her plate to avoid her grandad – across from her, still and silent.

'And so who was it you were out with?' says her gran.

Mum laughs. She says, 'Oh. Here it comes.'

'Here what comes?'

'Here it comes, you poking your beak into my business,' says Mum.

'It's my business when you're under my roof,' says her gran. 'And when it's my granddaughter you're taking out with you and strange men.'

Mum clucks. 'So she's your granddaughter now? This is your granddaughter that you've seen as many times in her whole life as I can count on one hand?'

'That's not fair. That's not how it was,' her gran says. She looks at the girl. She says, 'That wasn't how it was, pet.'

The girl looks at Mum and her gran closes her eyes and wraps her fingers around her mug. This circle.

'Oh come on,' says Mum. 'Let's just have a good meal together for once, eh? How's your shed getting on, Dad?'

'It's fine,' he says.

'The shed's getting on fine,' says Mum. 'And how are your pals getting on? How's Barbara?'

'Barbara's fine.'

'Barbara's fine!'

'And how was your holiday? I never even found out where you got to?'

No one answers, and in that spare moment the girl starts. She talks about the drive down and hearing about DiFranco's and she says the word *caravan* and Mum's cutlery clangs against the plate as it falls from her hands.

Her mouth hangs open. 'What did you just say?'

'What?' says the girl.

'Did you just say the caravan? *His* caravan?'

'What?' says the girl, looking around, something rising.

'Were you at Robert's caravan?' asks Mum.

Her grandparents are only just there – they're almost vanishing.

'Aye,' she says. 'Him and Aunty Pat's.'

And then Mum's standing up and backing across the kitchen and her gran's standing too.

'You took her *there*? To his…To that *fucken* caravan?'

Gran tells Mum to listen, but she won't – she's losing it fast.

Her grandad gets up and disappears into their bedroom and Mum's banging banging banging on the door.

'You can't walk away from me, Dad. No more do you walk away from me.'

No one sees the girl slip from the room. They're too busy to see her zip her coat as she moves, closing the front door behind her with no noise. She places a camera in the air that tracks her as she steals across the garden, over the dim street. The lens watches her advance into emptiness. Later on she'll watch the footage and see that she was not to blame.

Already it's Thursday.

146

AS SHE WALKS THE STREET SHE BURIES HER chin in her coat and steps back from the argument. It fades and is unremembered. Above her the sky melts and streams of feathered cloud point the way.

She gets the lads outside Chris's bit and they leave at once. Ally keeps flashing the neck of the bottle out of the top of his rucksack and they're all nearly skipping with the thrill of it. When they get to the beach, Chris and Darryl pull over some logs of driftwood and sit down. The first few pricks of starlight are starting to show through the sky and the ocean delivers its first lick of nipping air.

Chris is beside her and she can feel his heat through his anorak.

Ally fumbles with the bag and pulls forth the bottle. 'You're all very fucken welcome,' he says. 'I'm your knight in shining armour.'

They pass it around and marvel.

'It's almost like it's hot,' says Darryl.

Chris unscrews the bottle and smells. 'Ya bastard!'

All the boys have a drink and they make a show of it not affecting them, shaking their heads and saying you can't even taste it.

'You sure that's got alcohol?' says Darryl. 'It just tastes like juice.'

'It is a bit like juice,' says Ally. 'But then I'm used to the stronger stuff.'

When it's her turn, she accepts the bottle and holds it to her mouth. The smell reaches her nostrils and her sinuses shiver.

Swallows and gags and throat burns.

She says, 'Jeezo.'

Then everyone's laughing. She's passed the bottle a few more times. It burns in her belly, makes her light and heavy together – sleepy eyes.

The sound of waves chopping.

Lights moving in the woods above the beach.

Darryl and Chris race back and forth between the logs and the tide, falling into the sand when they reach the girl, running how you run in dreams. The moon pumps out cold light and Ally rests a torch against a log.

'We should've brought something to play music on,' says Ally, after some quietness. 'I'm really into my music. I was supposed to be going to see this band through in Glasgow the other weekend with my big cousins but it just never happened in the end. They got me a ticket and everything but I just never went. Are you?'

'What?'

'Into your music?'

'Aye,' she says.

'What bands do you like?'

'Oh,' she says, trying to remember. 'All sorts.'

'Right,' says Ally. 'Amazing. Me too. I've listened to all of these albums – my cousins get me into them. I love that sort of thing. You should come round and we could listen to some of that stuff. I've got these speakers now.'

'And the others?'

'Or just you.'

Darryl nearly falls into the water and Ally and the girl finish the bottle.

'Do those bother you?' he says, pointing to the crutches in the sand.

The girl shakes her head and it keeps shaking after she means it to.

'It's just I sometimes think they bother some folk. I sometimes see folk looking at them or my legs or whatever.'

'No,' she says.

'Nah, I didn't think you were bothered about them but I just thought I should ask in case. So what do you think about maybe coming round one time and we could try out those speakers I was saying about? It's not a big deal if you don't fancy it.'

'Eh?' she says. Is he asking about the crutches still?

'I mean – it's fine if you're not into it. It's not a big deal, like I was saying. I was just asking for a laugh really. Thought it might be fun but we can easily not bother.'

And the other two are storming up the sand behind her, pushing each other and laughing and Chris rushes up and pulls her back so it's like she's falling and her legs cycle the air ...

...and then it's later on and they're starting to build a fire. They sacrifice one of the logs and lay it down over a hole filled with dry seaweed. Chris gets the seaweed going and the log starts to blacken. The girl looks into

149

the embers until her eyes lose focus. Chris sits beside her in the sand. Her mind is wrong. It's slow and the connections are wrong. She wants to tell the boys about Mum, about what she's like and how it makes her feel.

Tide moves through shingle and sand, kindling crackles in the fire's hole.

The sky is silent.

The drink makes the girl ... Ideas wash onto and into her from the front. Of Mum searching the house, looking for her. And ...

...showing this other thing too, from before.

Her face is down against the carpet, at home, watching the orange bars of the electric fire and being so near to it that she needs to close her eyes to protect them from the heat.

'Get down,' Mum's saying and holding onto the girl's ears, holding them closed, but she's still hearing. Hearing the thumps and kicks at the front door, the letterbox rattling.

'Let me in, Angie,' says the voice outside.

The curtains are closed and the lights are off. Only glow is from orange fire-bars and tiny red LED blinking on the telly's front.

Her mother checks down the hallway from the floor and sees the person's still there, still ramming against the door.

'Fucken let me in,' the voice shouted. 'I've got to speak to Chloe.'

That's what the drink and the burning driftwood show her – lying on the carpet and hearing through Mum's fingertips that name being shouted through a letterbox.

The voice leaves and Mum sicks up in the toilet and

they don't put the telly back on all night, just in case. Instead they read stories in Mum's big bed and Mum keeps going out into the hallway to check.

'I'll be fucken back,' the voice had said.

And who was it? A boyfriend? Someone bad?

She's shaken, she tips.

She says, 'What?'

'There she is,' says Darryl, putting her…

…upright. And she's back by the fire and they're all peering in at her.

'Are you alright?' says Chris.

She nods, tastes sick a little. 'Fine.'

'She's grand,' says Ally. 'Leave her alone. So are we playing or not?'

'What's the game?' she says.

'What else?' says Darryl. 'Truth or bloody dare!'

They move the logs around in a circle so that they can still get the fire's heat and all eyes meet and Ally says, 'Who's going first?'

Darryl.

Ally says for him to run to the water and back with no trousers or pants and it's like he's been just waiting for the chance. He wriggles free of his lower clothing and throws them in the sand. Off he sprints and you can see his pale legs as he goes but you look away when he returns.

'Wow,' he says – the sound of clothing's friction as it's pulled on. 'What a rush! Who's next?'

'Me,' says the girl.

'Alright,' says Chris. 'So that'll be a truth then. Let's see – '

'No,' she says. 'Dare.'

A rumble flows through the boys. They're smiling and

rubbing palms and Ally clicks his fingers. 'You've got to jump over the fire.'

She looks at him though the heat's morphing. 'No. That's boring.'

Ally peers.

'I dare you to get off ...' says Darryl, 'with Chris.'

Nothing moves. Everyone watches.

The drink's made her mouth dry and her eyes swimmy. There's sand in the tender spaces between fingers. Trying to stand shows blurred lines of moving stars and to the one side woods. Then she's kissing Chris and she's using her mother's mouth, with its powerfulness, with its lipsticks. You can taste the booze but stronger, the sourness of your own mouth returning, doubled.

She's a foot taller, she's ten years older.

They break apart and his face zooms out from staring eyes and she can see Ally over his shoulder.

'Wow,' says Darryl.

Chris swallows and they both sit on logs.

'I never thought that would happen,' says Darryl, looking around, pleased with outrage.

'No,' says Ally. 'I never either.'

There's a moment of no talking and then Chris says, 'Who's next?'

'Ally's next,' says Darryl.

'I might just head up the road actually,' Ally says. His face has gone all narrowish. He isn't meeting eyes.

'Don't be like that,' says Chris.

'Like what?' says Ally.

Chris shrugs. 'Well.'

'I might just head up the road, cause I don't feel like hanging around with dirty wee s—'

But he doesn't finish. He stops himself and holds onto something unseen.

She can feel what's he's thinking though. What his mind spoke.

'Fine,' he says. 'One dare then I'll go. I'm not drunk anyway, who gives a shit?'

'Dare?' says Darryl.

'Aye,' he says. 'Why not?'

The numbers she's counting flow through her. There aren't any sounds, just numbersnumbersnumbers, then she says it: 'Go in the water.'

'What?'

'Go in the water,' she says, smirking. '*Swim.*'

He gets to his feet, cast from orange, and sniffs a little.

'You aren't going in the water,' says Chris. 'She's not being serious.'

'Aye she is, and aye I am. What's the problem? You think I've never been in the water before? I go swimming all the time with my other mates.'

Chris tries to hold him but Ally shrugs him off, hobbling along crutchless and he looks very young. Darryl covers his eyes and Chris is standing up and following and hot smoke is on her skin and in her clothes and makes her lips waxy as she licks them.

'Aye,' he calls. 'A nice swim. That'll be grand. A nice swim then home. How long?'

'Eh?' she calls back.

'I said how long are you wanting me in the fucken *water* for?'

'Don't go in,' she says. 'I was just—'

'OK, a quick dook,' he calls. 'Lovely.'

They follow him down to the edge and he shuffles in with shoes and jeans on and gets in up to the knees. He shrugs to them: What? On he goes, creeping deeper into the sea, swinging arms, sort of shouting now and then and crouching over slightly from when underfoot gets difficult. His arms are so thin that he holds them out of the water, near his head, as in surrender.

'Just come back in,' she calls. 'That's plenty.'

'Fuck off,' he sings.

He slips on shingle in the surf and then he's on his hands and knees, the black water lapping at his neck and his hair's plastered to his skull from the chops and foam of the water's angry movement. He tries to swim and his head goes in and out of the water like a bobbing cork. He gets further out and his face is just this one white smear among the caps and froth. It looks like he's laughing and then somehow his top's come off and whole moments go past when you can't tell if he's above the water or below it.

And it's all so fast and already he's going and the three of them plunge into the water and it's colder than you can imagine and heavier and impossible to fight against.

Someone shoves past her and there's a man there and a dog in the water and she doesn't know where they've come from. The man gets Ally back onto the beach and lies him down and the dog's soaking and licking Ally all over the face.

'What's going on?' moans the man. He's trying to hold Ally's head up and slap the dog away. 'I was only walking the fucken dug!'

Ally lies on the sand, sparkling, ribs slick and jeans solid-dark. The girl's throat vibrates. The three of them look at each other as the man does something with his mouth on Ally's mouth.

'Is that how it works?' the man's asking. 'Is that how it works?'

He does the thing again and looks up at them. 'Where's the ambulance?'

'It's coming now, John,' says a woman's voice, and the girl turns to see this lady's turned up and is twisting a mobile in her hands and nearly crying.

The man pushes down on Ally's pigeon chest and inside the girl feels the pressure herself.

Darryl squats down with a grimace.

The dog's managed to get past the man and it's licking Ally's face and he's trying to cough and you can see he's shit himself from all this brown smear going up his back and soon the beach is coloured by massive lights and the girl looks right into them as they go on and off, on and off: endless.

She puts herself down on the bed and rubs at her eyes with the balls of her palms. She delivers a flurry of light smacks to her temples and jaw. Once she's done with that, she looks around. This isn't what she expected at all; she was waiting for anger, not an empty house and the upstairs neighbour.

The front door closes and you can hear Karen waiting on the other side of the door. A soft knock. 'Can I come in?'

The door seems so far – the carpet stretches. The girl says, 'Aye.'

'Your wee pal,' she says. 'The boy – is it Alistair? With the crutches? They were saying he was in the water?'

The girl nods.

'What happened? They wouldn't say.'

'It was … Mum was having an argument and it was

about my uncle. It was ... I don't know, so I went to see the lads. Then there was, well, someone brought some drink.'

Karen has her hand on the girl's thigh. She says, 'Just take your time.'

'And he – I don't know. He went in the water and he couldn't swim, because of the ... you know.'

Karen exhales. The girl can smell her when she's close and the smell is of Parma Violets. 'Some night,' she says and brings the girl in for cuddling. 'It's not your fault – Jesus, it's not. Stuff like that there's no helping. Everyone has a drink and then accidents happen ... What's going on in there?'

She looks to where Karen's pointing: the girl's chest. She looks into that space and it opens out to be a blackness.

'Here's the truth for you. Life's hard enough for lassies. Our deck's stacked bad from the off. You have to work out what you feel. Not what you think you're supposed to or what people want you to. That's the most important thing. Someone told me that.'

Karen's dimples, when she smiles, are thick grooves in her cheeks and are soft with foundation. The girl's close to them and cannot deserve them. She says, 'I should get to bed,' and there's a jerk of surprise that goes over those dimples.

'Your gran and grandad came up. They wanted someone to be here when you got back. They've been out looking for you.'

'Alright,' says the girl, and she lies down on the bed and pretends to sleep and she feels Karen loiter for a minute or two before she goes out. Later, there's warm breath on her neck, but when the girl turns there's only the wall. She sleeps in her smoky jeans and T-shirt and there's water in her dreams. She has boils sprouting on her thighs and they resolve out into these little green buds like tree blossom in spring. Up to her knees in water and the boils, the buds, run up the legs to her T-shirt line. She twists one off and it flakes in her hand.

'But is she alright?' her grandmother's asking, in the real world. 'Have you checked?'

'She's not herself,' says Karen. 'Something's—'

And there's this sound, this agitation of clothing, and you can feel bodies wrangling and the door opens up: her grandad, bursting in.

'You awake?' he says.

She moves, only just.

'We will have words,' he says.

In the morning she has none of the bravery to leave the room. She counts over and over for what feels like hours and it's her need to pee that drives her out. Sat on the toilet, she stretches the fabric of her knickers between ankles. Maybe if she stays there long enough, until her legs are falling asleep from the seat, then when she goes out it'll be a different house she emerges into. She flushes and gets up to look at herself in the mirror, sees that smudges of ash are on her. She washes her face and leaves a dark ring of smoke round the edge of the basin. Every so often she remembers Chris's mouth on hers and the memory is strange and out of focus. When it comes to her, she pushes it down.

They're waiting for her in the kitchen.

'How're you doing?' says her gran.

'Fine,' she says. 'Where's Mum?'

Her gran doesn't give an answer. 'They said you were picked up drunk last night and that wee Alistair almost drowned.'

157

'I wasn't drunk,' she says. 'Not really.'

Her gran laughs. 'I've heard that before.'

Grandad coughs his watery cough, like an engine starting in the rain. All the softness has gone from his face and he says, 'Like mother, like daughter.'

'It wasn't my fault,' says the girl.

'Well,' says her gran. 'But the thing is, is you shouldn't be in those kinds of situations in the first place. Am I wrong?'

'Where's Mum?' she says.

Her grandad brings up his insect eyes. 'Gone off,' he says. 'Again.'

The girl leans back on the bunker. 'Why? What was the thing about Uncle Bobby?'

'We're not going to talk about that just now,' says Gran. 'We can talk about that when—'

Before she can finish, the girl goes out and into her room and closes the door hard enough to let them know. Throws open the curtains and allows in the burst of light that's waiting, then begins opening drawers and pulling clothes out onto the unmade bed. She finds her rucksack in the bottom of the wardrobe.

What's the story? asks the room. You off?

No, she says as she folds clothes and stuffs them down into the bag.

What is it then? asks the room.

I just want to be ready.

She comes to the dress her grandmother bought her and holds it against herself and sees that's what they want her to be – the girl who will fit a dress of cream paisley, of silks. She slips the dress back into the drawer, then remembers the magazine and the coin and lifts the mattress to find them. She rolls the magazine up and stuffs it into the

158

rucksack too and crams her bag beneath the bed.

A crack on the door: knuckles.

'In case it wasn't obvious,' says her grandad, through the wood, 'you are going nowhere.'

Good. Just disappear. Maybe a bus to anywhere. You could do that. A person could step up onto a bus and if you had the fare you could go wherever the bus was going. There was Edinburgh and Glasgow and even England and after that there was the whole rest of the world. She could disappear and they would say: we should have appreciated her while we had the chance.

But when you got there ... What then? That was the big question, what life was beyond your family and beyond the school.

Chris and Darryl are waiting outside when she answers the door. She checks behind herself and steps down onto the path.

'How is he?' the girl asks.

Chris says, 'Alright, I think. Our mums took us down the hospital. He's got a tube coming out his nose and another one putting medicine in his arm. It keeps him asleep but his mum's going spare.'

'Right,' says the girl.

Over and above, the sound of her grandad's noisy work, coming from the shed. The girl looks at the path. Between its slabs, furry heads of dandelions poke through among bursts of grass. Beneath her foot is the stem of something. She lifts it to find the head of a dandelion, crumpled, gone to seed. Bits of its fluff drift and flutter away from her raised foot like the down of tiny birds. Warmth bleeds from the slabs, through her sandals, bleeds from the building's pink walls.

Chris touches his nose. 'Will you have to go back?' he asks.

'Maybe,' she says. 'Mum had to get home for work, so she never found out, thank God.'

She can feel something coming – inside and out. There's a train pummelling down the valley of her insides. There's string leading from her belly and she's itching from the dreamed buds on her thighs.

Both boys look up and then her gran's at the stair top, arms folded.

'Come back another time,' she says and they slope off across the garden.

She's waiting for the ability to vanish. Lying on top of the bed, the heat burning itself out and the window allowing in the smells of baking leaves and tarmac, she's willing herself to melt. She shows herself her grandparents dancing on the living room rug and in the memory it's a silly thing, the pair of them doddering and clumsy. In the memory she laughs at them. She shows herself Karen looking down from the window and you can see how she's all fat around the middle and how the uniform bulges where her trousers pinch. She shows herself Ally bobbing in black water and he's such a baby that the girl has to switch him off.

She lies still and clenches and prays to float – she sends a bird of herself skyward to leave behind this scrap and the sky-swimming girl meets its mother and the cameras she places in clouds show them merging like white hands.

At night, the phone goes in the hallway. Her gran brings it through and says, 'It's your mum again. She's home. Do you want to speak to her?'

160

The girl wrestles it away, holds the cup to her mouth. 'Hello?'

'Is she there?' says Mum. 'Your gran? Say yes if she is.' 'Yes.'

'OK. Don't say anything else. Listen: I'm outside on the mobile. Give it half an hour and come. We're going.'

'Alright,' says the girl. 'Fine.'

Gone.

She hands the receiver back and her gran searches her for something. Finding it missing, she closes the door and lights go off.

You sure this is a good idea? the room asks.

She grunts as she stretches to reach the bag. Aye, she says. She gets it by the top handle and pulls it out.

It's just, says the room, what happens if she loses it again?

It'll be different, she says.

She checks inside the drawer and sees the dress is still in there, folded up neat. The material is slippy as she runs it between her fingers.

She closes the drawer.

Someone comes down the hall and the weight in the steps says it's her grandad. She can see him through the open door. He pauses outside the toilet, touching the handle. There's no way he can hear her, she's standing so still, breathing these tiny breaths through her nose. He looks over his shoulder. He looks at the girl. He looks at the girl and the rucksack on her shoulder and then he nods.

She can hear her grandfather's rattling breath and his piss filling the toilet bowl as she exits the house and the beaded curtain makes almost no noise as she opens and closes the front door.

Parked by the kerb is a car with its lights on. She comes

up to the passenger window and sees that it's Mum and Stig inside the car. They don't notice her because they're facing away.

The girl counts to five. In that space, she wonders, what happens in the next world? What happens after you disappear?

She taps on the glass with her nail and both heads snap to face her. Mum covers her mouth and when she takes it away she's smiling. Rolls down the window. 'We were waiting on you.'

The girl counts again. 'OK.'

Stig reaches across Mum to shake hands. 'It's Stig,' he says and the girl says she remembers. 'Very cool,' he says.

All the time the girl's watching Mum and it's like hypnosis. It's like a balm. What happened when you disappeared was that someone was there to look after you.

A gurgle from the back. The girl looks and sees a baby in a car seat.

'That's Stig's boy,' says Mum. 'Declan McDonald.'

'McDonald's his mum's name,' says Stig.

The girl looks at the baby, wriggling in his sleep. 'Right,' she says.

'So,' says Mum. 'Are you coming?' The circles of her eyes look upwards to the girl and are clear and healthy and are saying for her not to be afraid. Saying to her: this is what happens next.

She gets in the back beside the baby.

After a few seconds, peering up at the house, Mum tells Stig to go and then they're gone.

Mum leans to the side and faces the girl. 'Sorry it took so long to come back,' she says. 'Me and Stig had to sort some stuff out first, had to pick up Declan. But we're here now. All of us together. A family.'

Her hand creeps between the seats and squeezes the girl on the knee, so that warmth can enter her there and seep up her body.

'A family,' confirms Stig.

'How long is it to get home?' she asks.

Mum winks at her. She says, 'We're not going back there. Too many bad vibes. Too much mess. We're cleaning up – going someplace much better.'

As they leave town and join the carriageway, Mum gets out the mobile to make a call.

'Hello,' she says, and the girl sees her face's skin become sharp, so she knows it's her grandmother on the other end. 'Listen, I know, I know,' says Mum. 'I'm not calling for any of that. I'm just saying I've taken her back. That's us off home again, so don't worry about us, OK?'

The mobile makes a fuzz sound but you can't make out exact words.

'I already said to you I'm not talking about any of that stuff. You shouldn't have taken her down the caravan. That was—'

'…'

Mum laughs without any joke in her voice. 'You *would* say that. But anyway, it's a pointless discussion – I've taken her back and she's my child so that's the end of it. Goodbye, nice to speak to you.'

She puts the mobile into the gap behind the handbrake and sighs.

She's jolted out of sleep as they pull over, up onto the embankment, the car rocking from the land's roughness.

It's night now. She's slept right through the journey and the land is wild – nothing is lit in the dark.

'Fuck,' says Stig, turning to see the back window. 'What was that?'

'That was an animal,' says Mum, looking round too. 'Was it?'

The girl twists in her seat and sees the road curve behind them, coloured red by Stig's brake lights.

'It came right out in front of us,' says Stig. 'It was kind of flying, I don't know.'

If she twists her neck she can just about see this shape further back on the road. Something making a shadow.

'Hold on,' says Mum and opens her door with a rush of cool air. She walks back in the embers of the lights, stray hairs glowing.

Stig mumbles to himself. 'What's she doing? What's she doing?'

You can make out slivers of gold in the mess on the road, areas of feathered sheen, and it's moving a little bit too. Mum creeps closer and puts hands to hips – one person out there, all red, all alone. She combs her hair with her fingers. Doesn't look back. Raises a foot and brings it down hard onto the shape, heavy. Once, twice, another. She's almost jumping into the mess and Stig lets out a breath. After it's over, she crouches down to peer into her creation, then nods.

The girl watches Mum come back, holding her hand up to shield herself from the lights, sort of squinting.

First, she wipes her trainers on the embankment. 'Put it out its misery,' she says, climbing back inside. 'This bird.'

BY DAY THEY'RE DRIVING THROUGH A landscape of low hills, long slopes that go all the way across, as far as you can see. No houses, no flats, no shops – just hills and a whole world the girl's never entered before.

She woke in the car just as the brightness began and everyone else was already awake. Had to pee down the ditch at the side of the road and they ate crisps and Babybels for breakfast. Mum plays twinkling songs on the car's stereo to match the sunshine and even the baby's showing off his gums.

'Not long now,' Stig announces.

Here's a little white house emerging from the glenside and here's the car leaving the main road for the track and here's Stig bringing the car up outside the house. The girl can hear water running through the window and shiny knots of birdsong come down from the sky.

'What is it?' she asks.

'It's my boss's place,' Stig says, killing the engine. 'My old boss.'

'It's perfect,' says Mum, her voice rising.

'You wait here,' says Stig, climbing out. 'I'm needing to see something.'

He jogs around the back of the house, his longish hair trailing behind him.

The girl and Mum get out and look at the house and Mum's hand is on her back. Before now, the furthest out the girl's been was a trip to a farm. The school had a minibus to get them there and you had to wander around and see the animals from a distance and have the farmer tell you what a difficult life it was. You had to wear wellies because of the mud and shit that was everywhere and you didn't even get to touch a single animal – not one. People brought lunches from home but the girl and a few others got them free off the school. Not much fun really, except a dog came snarling out of a doorway and made Abbie McMurdo fall down with her hands in the mud but the dog was tied to a chain anyway so that the rest could laugh.

The front door opens and out comes Stig.

'Only had a key for the back,' he shouts over. 'Let's roll.'

Inside the house smells like cleaning stuff and wood. It's all shiny and brown and the floor isn't carpets – it's wood too.

'Where's Declan?' asks Stig.

Mum prances down the hallway and looks back from the living room door. 'In the car I suppose?'

'Christ,' Stig goes, barging past.

'This is the life,' says Mum, kicking her legs in the air, pulling the girl down into the big brown leather couch. They wriggle their fingers together against the leather and breathe in the cleanness and they're doing smiles, smiles,

166

smiles. Declan gets laid out on a playmat in the middle of the room and Stig brings in carrier bags of food from the car and down into the kitchen.

Mum wiggles her mobile as he passes. 'There's no bars.'

'No,' he laughs. 'Course not. There's no reception out here.'

'Why isn't there?'

Stig pauses. 'I mean, it's the country, Angie. You don't often get signal.'

She looks at the mobile. 'You could have said something.'

'I thought you'd know.'

'Right, OK. But you should've said something. That's just politeness.'

'There's a landline if you need it.' The bags are heavy and Stig has to change arms to redistribute the weight.

'Is there a computer at least?' asks Mum and baby Declan starts to grumble.

Stig's made his way into the kitchen and he pops his head back up. 'I told you there's not,' he says.

The girl gets up and goes out into the hallway and climbs the stairs. They lead to a small upper hall with two bedrooms leading off. In the smaller she puts her rucksack down on the bed and opens the curtains. There's all this stuff about the room that shows you someone lives there. There's toys on the windowsill and swimming certificates Blu-Tacked over the bed.

From the window though ... Nothing between her and the raw open world except glass. Silver veins of burn appear up on the hillside among the violet brush and the sky is a mussel shell – colour bleeding into pure blankness. Downstairs the baby's crying, but if she closes the door she can't hear it. There's a ringing sound in her ears that when she concentrates is the sound of Mum and Stig fighting.

One two three – one two three.

One two three.

The telly's on and Mum has Declan up on her chest and he's buried into her neck. There's a flower of shards on the kitchen floor, spread out in a circle from the bottom pane of the back door.

'Mind that glass,' shouts Stig. 'My boss forgot to leave the keys so ... Aye. Mind the glass.'

She wants to look inside the carrier bags slumped on top of the kitchen bunker, see what food's going. But the rustling ...

She'll count and then ask.

She counts, and then, 'Is there anything for lunch?'

Angry movements up in the living room – footsteps storming over.

Mum appears at the top of the stair. 'Can you just wait a minute? Jesus. We're trying to get the bairn settled.'

'Alright,' says the girl. 'Sorry.'

Mum gives her one of those looks.

They take the path into the hills and the wind is empty with no taste. Stig walks with Declan in a sling over his chest. They stop to rest at the top of the nearest hill and Mum lights a fag and blows it away from the baby's face.

'Look at this,' says Stig. He has a map of the land they're in. He spreads it out onto the ground and points to somewhere. 'That's where we are.'

It's greenness and brownness all around them on the map. In the top corner there's a smaller map of the whole country with a red square to show that's what the bigger map shows.

'Wow,' says the girl – all these places.

'It's my ambition to visit every one of these squares of the country,' Stig tells her, over the tuft of his son's head. He flips it over and you can see he's coloured in loads of the map's squares.

'Wow,' she says again and picks it up for a closer look.

'Put that down,' says Mum. 'You're going to rip it.'

She puts it down.

'What a view,' says Stig, pointing the way they've come, down towards the house and the road and the fields beyond.

They keep going until they reach what Stig calls a *deer fence*, only there's no deer to be seen. The path kinks and leads them up to the top of a second, larger hill. Fat smudges of gorse are like yellow fires in the sunlight and she notices that rabbits scurry between them. As her eyes rummage the landscape it appears still and solid but when she concentrates on one area it comes alive with movement. Flowers and tall grasses twist and flicker and rabbits flash white arses.

'Let's get back,' says Mum.

'Just a bit longer,' says Stig. 'There's something up here.'

You come up onto the crest of this hill and way beyond the fields and meadows there are dark spikes at the furthest you can see.

'What are those?' she asks.

'Those are the real bad mountains,' Stig says. 'I've climbed one or two myself and they're actual terrors.'

When the dark comes, Stig closes the curtains and gets the beer out. Declan sleeps on the playmat and there's not much talking and, when there is, it's about people the

169

girl doesn't know. It's fine, because they're a family now. There's Mum and here's the girl and they're watching telly together after a walk in nature. You could look at this scene from outside and you would know it was happiness.

Stig pulls the playmat away and pushes the coffee table up between the two couches and sets up the Cluedo board. The girl's the purple one. Plum.

'Maybe I'm the murderer,' giggles Mum. 'Maybe I'm going to murder Stig, with a gun, in the brain!'

Stig thinks this is so funny. He slaps the coffee table and nearly spits his beer out.

The girl's needing a six on the dice. Her mind tells the dice to be a six as it falls, and it's a six.

'Nice one,' goes Stig as he comes back from the kitchen with more beers.

'That's enough games for tonight,' says Mum, opening a can.

'Ah,' says Stig. 'It's a laugh though.'

'Aye,' says the girl. 'Come on, Mum.'

Mum purses her lips. 'I'd say it's time for someone's bed.'

The bedroom here doesn't speak. The girl's all alone in there. But it's alright, because she can make herself vanish, she can let herself leak into the walls and land.

Her brain wants her to see the boys. It's the sounds at first – their calling and shouting in the woods, their joking and teasing. You can hear their noises of pleasure as they destroy the wasteground – the rasping burst of wood being torn from wood, rocks and bricks splintering in collision. Then their faces start to leak through and Darryl's kneeling down to kiss the tree lovingly and she's smiling. The three of them on the grass and her peering over the fence to see their construction and then the stone hurtling towards her. Ally's making these inching steps out onto a branch, his hands and crutches reaching for purchase, shards of bark falling. They're on the beach and she has Chris beside her, this hard weight by the fire, and she's sliding up to him ...

She can't see this. It's not possible to see this. She sweeps the curtains closed and goes to bed and makes herself sore from trying to sleep. In time, she manages – she's asleep, until she isn't anymore and it's hours later and there's those famous shagging sounds from the next room over. A bed being shunted, this sort of crying.

The clock shows four ... but it's fine. The girl doesn't mind. She gets her head under the duvet and breathes her own breath again and it's just like when she was younger, back home. She's done it before and she can do it a million times if she has to. Inside the duvet's like inside a cloud – aye – it's like she's within this cloud that's bobbing along through skies and seeing marvels below. It's moist and smelly but there's nothing beneath her feet for miles and miles.

The crack of a baby's laugh.

She throws back the sheets and there's a travel cot at the end of the bed and Declan's standing up inside, looking and laughing in the dark.

This is fine. Just wave at him. Make him feel safe.

He starts to cry when he sees the girl.

'No,' she whispers, creeping along the bed to loom over him. 'Shush. Please.'

It doesn't help.

Maybe they'll hear him and come through. The girl counts to see. They don't come and his crying is sharp and sore. She can see his cheeks are stained cherry-red and so she pads the two steps across the hall, knocks gently on the other door. The noise coming through is vigorous and damp.

'What is it?' Mum asks.

'Declan's crying.'

'See to him then.'

A spasm of anger runs up her neck like toothache and she has to force it down.

She holds him up under the armpits and he's heavier than she expected and he wriggles like a dog. She grips him to her front and he screeches right into her earhole. The holding him up doesn't help, so he must be sick. He has these worms in his belly and blood is trickling through the spaces inside him. She can see the infection in his spinal column, in the fluid of his heavy crying head. She knows the things that can go wrong from the Body Book and Declan has them all – she knows he's going to give one last squawk and his body will fall limp as his wee soul slips from the window.

One, two, three. One, two, three.

'Shush. Sh-sh-shush,' she tells him, rocking with each shush. His cries go on and on and all the time he's pushing against her, rejecting her wholly.

You cannot do this, he tells her. You cannot control me.

Mum bursts in then, fastening her dressing gown. Doesn't say a word, just hoists him away from the girl and slams the door shut behind herself.

The girl goes back to bed and her skin has pain from the force he used on her.

Everyone's sleeping when she goes downstairs. All across the floor are crumpled beer cans and the saucers they've been using for ashtrays. Stig's taped some cardboard over the broken window and swept up most of the glass but a few shards glisten in the gap between the door and floorboards. Just beers in the fridge but she finds bread and jam in one of the carrier bags.

She carries her breakfast through and sinks into the couch and now here's Stig thumping down the stairs after her, his long hair and beard greasy and curly. Declan under his arm.

'Morning,' he says, passing into the kitchen for tea and baby formula.

He's an alright sort, this Stig – compared to some of the others anyway. His face moves slow but it doesn't make him look dumb. He knows how to make people feel safe and his stomach looks comfortable on him. She feels the cushion rise as his weight flops down beside her.

'Sorry about this one last night,' he says, holding up the bottle so that the bairn can drink from it. 'If it means anything, I said he should come in with us.'

The bairn watches the girl over the bottle's bottom as he chugs.

She says, 'He was fine.'

'No,' says Stig, 'he wasn't.' He moves baby Declan to the other elbow and turns on the telly to check the time. 'Want to see something cool?'

She nods.

'Meet me out the back in ten. This one's needing changed and so on.'

Face washed, hair in a plait. She ducks her head to spit mint foam into the sink. She turns her head side to side, juts out her jaw. People always said that you'd grown, how big you'd got and how fast it happened, but it seems slow from within. To her, she has the same face as baby

Declan. Her cheeks look chubby. She hates the skinniness of her neck, it's length. Overall, this is a wee lassie's face.

Stig takes longer than ten minutes to meet her, so she's left pacing over the head of the nearest hill. She makes Ls of her thumbs and fingers and puts the house into a photograph. The hillside is littered with holes and divots: rabbit houses. She hunkers down and looks into one of them and it leads into blackness. She pictures all of the hill's holes leading into a central den. There's another girl in there. She's down beneath her, suspended in the dirt like a baby in a belly, breathing through the rabbit holes. If she gets right down on her knees and up close to the opening of the hole, she can almost make out the faintest trace of...

'Haha!' yells Stig from behind, making her jump. 'Rabbits! Good thinking, but maybe we'll start off with something smaller?'

She's confused about the pole he has over his shoulder. 'Is that real?'

Stig nods with pride.

'How come you've got a gun?'

'Well, it's an air rifle, not a real *gun* gun.'

She remembers using Darryl's gun out on the waste-ground. It's a warm feeling to think of the boys but she forces away that warmth. She says, 'I've used one of them before. My mate at my gran's had one.'

'Oh aye?' says Stig. 'Did it look like this?'

'Kind of,' she says. 'Maybe smaller. Sort of like—' She makes the shape.

'Very good,' he says and she realises her face is doing something that she twists it out of.

Stig hands her Declan and jogs to the next hill and back, setting up soup tins and beer cans in a row.

'Watch this,' he says, lying on his front.

The rifle is long and the barrel shines with an oily slickness. 'Pow,' he says and the crack and its echo come both at once and the can furthest to the left somersaults over itself. He shows her how to snap the rifle in two and push one of the pellets down into the barrel.

'Line up the sights but mind and aim high and to the right,' says Stig.

The trigger's stiffer than she thought. It takes a hard tug to give and she loses her aim and fires the first pellet off into the openness.

'Shite,' she says. 'Sorry.'

'No worries. Have another shot.'

She manages to reload it herself. Her fingers are quivering.

'Just be still while you're aiming – don't breathe.'

She focuses and pushes all the breath from her body. Here's the can, here's the barrel. 'Pow,' she says and the middle one goes flying.

'Nice one. You glanced it off the side.'

She nods. Her ear nearest the gun rings.

Stig gets down too, letting Declan sit free on the grass. 'Can't wait till this one's old enough that I can show him stuff like this. Learn him to ride a bike and so on.'

'How's he not with his mum?'

He squints, pulls up some blades from the hill. 'She needed a break. Dead busy these days.'

'OK,' she says, recognising a fellow liar in this man.

'I can look after him. Folk say a bloke isn't suited for looking after bairns but that's rubbish.' He rolls up his T-shirt sleeve to show the girl a tattoo that reads:

DECLAN
MCDONALD
LIVES

The girl looks at these words, then says, 'I think Mum likes him.'

'Aw, she's great with kids, your mum. You're lucky. Mine was a nightmare. Dad too actually.'

'How do you know her – Mum?'

'Me and your mum? We were at the school same time – we go right the way back. I did Home Ec see? Do you choose your subjects yet? Naw? Well, when you do, you'll see that none of the lads do Home Ec. Except I did. Me and your mum used to do cakes and that – a genuine laugh. All flour on our faces and so on.' He chuckles at the memory. 'She was always fun.'

The girl starts to wonder ... Maybe it's *her* that's the problem. Too serious, folk used to say. Maybe Mum's just fun and the girl can't know it due to youngness, due to being a stick-in-the-mud. But anyway! It's not as though there's even a problem in the first place! She's happy, and here's Stig setting up more cans on the far slope.

'Right,' he shouts, jogging back across. 'This time get it right in the heart.'

She rolls over onto her front, breaks the gun, feeds it a pellet, and throws out a camera to swoop low over herself. Gets the can in her sights. Stops her breath. The grass below tickles. Insects scrabble in the roots. Zoom in on her narrowed eyes – one lid closes.

Pow.

The can flips and falls backwards in hysterics.

They high five and she's smiling and jumping on the spot and Mum's coming up from the house. Wipes the grin off her face while Stig turns and waves.

'What's going on?' Mum asks, looking at the gun and then at the two of them. She stands on tiptoes and gives

176

Stig one of those kisses and her eyes are open and looking at the girl as she does it.

'This one's a proper killer,' says Stig. 'Look: she got them cans.'

'How come you never woke me up?' asks Mum.

'I thought you wanted a lie in? To relax and so on?'

Mum pushes her tongue into her cheek, pupils snooker-balling between Stig and the girl. 'Aye? Really? If you say so.'

'I mean ... I'm sorry?'

'I suppose I'll just let you get on with it, if I'm not welcome.'

They cross to the other hill and collect the cans but he keeps glancing towards the house. The house has eyes and the house's eyes are Mum's eyes and Stig knows this too. When she's out of earshot, Stig says, 'Looks like I'm in the doghouse.'

After tea she gets the magazine from upstairs and reads it while the rest watch telly. The magazine has a quiz in it that tells you whether or not the boy you like fancies you. It has questions like: *DOES HE MAKE SPECIAL EFFORTS TO SIT CLOSE* BY?

But she can't remember ever sitting down with any of the boys, not in a chair anyway. She does remember Chris's eyelashes and the just-thickening of his forearms, sleeves sometimes pushed up there.

Stig pokes her in the leg with his toe from the next couch. 'What's that you've got there? Let me see ... What is this? *Is He Mr Right?*' he reads and then laughs, but in a kind way. 'Are you looking for Mr Right and so on? Who's he then? Who's your boyfriend?'

She smiles and closes the magazine and goes to slap his foot with it.

'Pft,' goes Stig, kicking the magazine away. 'Here, do you know who the boyfriend is?' he asks Mum.

Mum looks up from the telly, scoffs. 'She's not got a boyfriend,' she says. 'Hardly.'

Stig's smile falters. 'I was just joking about.'

The girl wants to say something. Something about how she'd rather be quiet and not have a boyfriend than have all these boyfriends that make you cry and kick at the front door.

A scowl sharpens Mum's face. She turns to Stig. 'Why is it you're so interested anyway?'

'*Interested*? How am I interested?'

'Just why is it you're so fascinated by my daughter's love life all of a sudden?'

Stig looks around, looking for help from someplace. 'How am I fascinated, like? I was only having a mess about with her and so on!'

'You seem quite fascinated, Stig.'

The girl keeps her eyes on the magazine, studying the features of the healthy, wholesome girl on the cover. She's kind of photographed mid-turn at the waist, all these brownish hairs shining in rivers on shoulders and back.

'I'm just curious about that,' says Mum.

Stig's bamboozled and it shows up in his voice. 'I'm sorry. I wasn't meaning it in a—' he says, searching for the word, 'in a pervy way.'

'What?' screeches Mum, at once animated. '*Pervy*? Where's that coming from, pervy? Who said anything about perviness? How come that's come up all of a sudden?'

She's kind of half-standing now and holding out her arms.

Through the window and back door you can see the

hills behind and the flat land in front of the house and everything's these colours of nature against the evening sun. She thinks of the girl down there in the hill, hopes that rabbits don't bung up the tunnels and choke her air. If she could dig her up, she would.

The rest of the evening's spent watching telly in silence and drinking cans until Declan's needing his bed. Mum tells the girl he's coming in with her again. The girl says this is fine but asks, won't he cry though?

'Of course he'll cry – he's just wee. Or does Princess St Madame need her beauty sleep too much? Should we leave the wee mite in the cold?'

She nods.

Think of how she came to save you. Think of how she waited in the car, just so she could keep you by her side forever. Don't watch as Stig takes baby Declan upstairs for bed, focus on the telly so that you can't be ungrateful.

Mum's lighter sparks in the dimness of the corner. 'You're a clever one,' she chuckles. 'I'll give you that.'

The girl's neck prickles from needles of sweat.

'The magazine thing: dead smart. I'd never think of something like that.'

The girl says nothing back.

'Is it you think I'm daft? Is that it?'

'I don't think you're daft,' the girl tells the telly.

'You must think I'm daft if you're pulling the "look at me and my sexy magazine" nonsense, the "I'm a saucy wee lassie" trick.' Mum wiggles her fingers as she whispers. 'I hope you realise,' she adds, with an exasperated giggle, 'that there's no one else out there giving a shit about you except me.'

'People do,' says the girl.

'People do what?' her mother spits.

'Do give a ... do care about me.'

Her mother laughs and draws on the fag. 'Tell me. Who is it cares about you? Is it your granny and grandad? Your poor old grandparents that your mum treats so bad? Get some sense in your head, because they could not care less about you. It's me that's your mum. Who is it that's cooked and cleaned up after you and wiped your moaning arse all these years?'

Silence. Awareness of her whole body.

'Exactly,' says her mother. 'Thank you, very much.' She tips the can down her neck.

'No.' That's it, that's all she's got. *No.*

But her mother's ready. She leans in, snakes across the couch. 'No? *No*, is it? You want to know how come they were so keen to take you this summer? Was it cause they gave a shite? No. It was cause I was sending them twenty quid a week, out the child support. Twenty quid. That's it. That's all you were worth.'

Don't cry. Don't show her you crying. Just let the earth fall over you and be quiet and still. Ignore the lump in your neck, bite your tongue, bite your lip hard so it cannot tremble.

Mum leans her head sideways on her hand, resting both on the arm of the couch nearest the girl. 'Aw. Madame Princess's upset. Her big bad mum's upset her again, cause she isn't perfect every single time? What a cow she is? Is that it? But listen: at least I'm here with you. I'm the only cunt feeding you, *caring* for you out the goodness of my heart. Twenty quid – that's all it was.'

Breath one. Breath two. 'OK.'

Her mother lights up again and moves the fag's red dot around, appreciating her handiwork. The fag makes crinkling sounds as she uses it. Shakes her head. 'How come we can't just be – I don't know – just be friends? Like in the old days?'

She tries to hold it in, but there's no resolve left and over the couch she creeps. Mum opens her arms and the girl crawls to them, accessing the warmth of that tightness.

'I'm sorry,' she hiccups.

Across the room she was bald and alone but now she's up close and she knows she was wrong. She isn't alone anymore so it must be her mother who was right and there's something wrong with the girl, deep down in an essential corner of her insides. Forgive me. Take my head in your hands and see the rotten kernel in the middle of me – hold me anyway. They hug and the girl brings all the odours in through her mouth, through deep breaths – fags and the special perfume and this sweetness of skin that's the language all words come from.

In the ground of the night: here's the girl and the fizzling babymind of Declan McDonald, together in the dark. We're a family now, he tells her. We're in this together. Out they go into the hills, the ground and the sky coloured likewise. They hold hands and look back to the house – a glowing bone, a mushroom.

Shall we run away? wonders the babymind.

It could be done, says the girl.

The boils are back. She opens her jeans and they're all there on her thighs. Red boils that change and open into potato eyes and plant-life. She wants to wipe them off, to clean herself of them, but she's terrified they're a part of her and to remove them would cause pain. Fronds poke from the edges of her pants – sprouts of girl growing there when she didn't look, boils bursting into greenish leaf.

She turns away from the baby to check inside the

knickers, but before she can get a look, he's crying and it's muffled because he's down inside the earth. Then she's running because the ghost in the hill put him there and she's coming for the girl too, but she's tripping over the vines and tendrils growing from her middle and it's tearing the plant-life from her skin and it truly is pain.

His real crying wakes her and it's ages before she manages to get him down again. She is tired and this baby speaks long and loud screeches in the dark room and, when even herself is not observing, she nips his chubby arm.

HER MOTHER ROCKS HER AWAKE AND AS the girl cracks eyelids open, she leans over with a blurry grin.

She says, 'Morning, you.'

The girl sits up. Baby Declan's not in his cot. 'Morning.'

'How did you sleep?'

'Fine.'

'We took the bairn in with us in the end. Didn't seem fair to have him getting you up at all hours.'

The girl nods. 'Thanks.'

She follows her mother downstairs, where the kitchen's been cleaned and there's bowls and measuring jugs and a big sack of flour waiting for them on the worktop. The atmosphere of the night before has simply, completely *gone*.

'Pancakes,' explains Mum.

It's a messy business, making these. Flour gets sifted all down the cupboard doors and the mixer sprays a comb of batter up the wall.

'So the trick,' says Mum, 'is getting the consistency

right. Too thin and you'll end up with crepes, too thick and you get those great big mattress-sized things.'

The girl gives the batter a whirl – her spoon leaves behind a ghost of the mixture. 'How's that?'

'It looks grand. Did you know I used to make you these all the time, when you were wee. Do you mind?'

'Nope.'

'All the time. You liked them with bananas chopped inside.'

They serve them up and Stig and baby Declan come in from the garden and take their share and they all sit around and have breakfast together. The pancakes are good.

Stig collects the plates to do the washing up, but Mum touches him on the wrist. 'Let me get that.'

It must look nice, from the camera, through the window. This perfect family of a mum and a dad and the kids and them all sharing food on a morning. You couldn't get nicer than that, could you? But though – if it's nice, then why's there this ache in the girl's shoulder? Why can't she get any comfort from her chair? Why is she sometimes flinching?

Stig asks her what she wants to be after the school, but not in that way like Uncle Bobby – you can see he's actually interested.

'I don't know,' she says, truthfully.

'I could see you being an artist,' says Stig. 'You've got the right brain, I reckon. You need a good brain and so on to be one of them artists.'

'Maybe,' says the girl.

'What did you want to be, Angie?' he asks.

'When I was her age?' asks Mum from the sink.

'Aye.'

'I always thought I could be a good nurse. I always

thought I'd like it how they look after people and give them health again.'

'I always wanted to be a millionaire,' admits Stig.

'A millionaire? From what though?' asks Mum.

He just shakes his head. 'No idea, but it sounded good to say *I'm a millionaire*. A cool million? No worries! Just milkshakes, whenever I want them.'

'Milkshakes? You're soft in the head.'

'Are you kidding, Angie? Who wouldn't want milkshakes every single day of their life? You'd be a mug to pass that up.'

'We could rob a bank,' says Mum. 'Like Thelma and Louise.'

'They were both birds though.'

'Well, still. We could do that.'

'You're thinking of Bonnie and Clyde,' says Stig. 'They were a bird and a bloke and they robbed banks, only they got shot from it.'

'Never mind who it was. We could do it.'

Stig laughs. 'Aye, and we could use Declan here as a hostage. Like, give us all the dough or this wee baby gets it.'

'Aye?'

'Let's do it,' laughs Stig. 'We could split it fifty-fifty.'

'What about you?' asks Mum. 'Do you want in? You can be the getaway driver.'

'Aye,' says the girl. 'OK then.'

This moment is good, so live within it. Climb inside this moment and freeze yourself still, so that if it breaks you cannot be blamed.

Stig's sleeping on the couch. She tries to creep past but his eyes open fast as lights. He looks shocked. 'Oh,' he croaks, leaning up on an elbow and rubbing his face. 'Must've nodded off.'

She opens a cupboard in the kitchen. Empty. There's leftover beans in a can in the fridge. Those, microwaved in a mug for lunch. She sits on the opposite couch and spoons hot beans to her mouth as they watch the News and Weather. The News shows a photofit of a man that looks a bit like an older Darryl. He peers out, looking lost, looking missing. The weather shows that big red clouds are heading towards them on the map. The man says a storm's in the post.

'This is depressing,' says Stig and changes channels. 'How could anyone deal with all that stuff? All that proper stuff, and so on.' Stig nods and scowls and looks out the window. 'Here,' he says. 'Your mum. Is she OK?'

'How do you mean OK?'

'I mean *OK* OK.'

She shrugs, so he goes on.

'I mean, she was always – she was always different at the school, but in a good way. I'm not saying she was mental or anything. Like silly different. Always cracking jokes and playing the fool and so on and I loved it. You should have seen her in her day. Do you think she's maybe poorly or something?'

'I think she's fine.'

Stig watches her. 'Really? I thought so too, but sometimes—'

'I think she's fine.'

He nods, appears to be thinking it over.

She finishes the beans, scraping the bottom of the mug, and then baby Declan starts to cry on the floor above and they look to the ceiling. A few beats pass, then thumping footsteps going from one side to the other. You can feel her mother's annoyance even from through the plaster.

The girl gets up and washes her mug in the sink and in the sound of running water her grandparents start coming through. She tries to push them down but they resist, crowding into her mind. She plunges the mug into warm water and sees her grandfather on his knees, sawing wood, generating clouds of suspended dust and he's making the bird feeder for the garden. She sees her grandmother comparing loaves of bread and the girl's standing, holding the magazine at the end of the aisle. Three of them eating together around the little table, these heavy meals that weigh the girl down and make her sleepy with comfort.

There's this other life she exists within – her flesh is elsewhere too. And this other life is pulling on her atoms, saying to her that if she wants, she can return ... But no. She plunges the mug into water and washes it away, because that life is dead. She's in a family now and the most important thing is to hold that together – hold it together against any and all odds. A wave of clouds is coming onwards over the hills. She needs to keep her grandparents down, so she goes out the back in just socks to watch. You can taste it on your tongue, the storm. Clouds coloured deep and electric, bringing down the roof of the sky.

A single droplet of rain on her forehead.

More drops on her face, on her arms. Licks her lips, tastes her own skin and sweat. She stays out so she's soaked to the bone, so that nothing but this discomfort can live inside her. She trails wet footprints across the lino, the rain hammering on all the house's windows and it's like twilight through the glass, with these black and white ropes of rain worming across the pane. The noise helps to keep them from her – she cannot hear her grandfather's moist breath against the rain's drumming, cannot remember his radio that played reels and jigs on accordions.

After washing under the shower, she uses her mother's posh hair cream and her fingers run through her hair like thread. Cold air stings her face as she opens the door into the hall and she hops upstairs in a towel and roots around in her bag for clothes. She sniffs the armpit of one T-shirt and it's not too bad and there's a pair of jeans right down the bottom of the rucksack. She thinks of the dress Gran got for her.

But no – she cannot picture the dress, or her gran picking it out for her, or her gran going into the bedroom after the girl left and opening the drawer to see it lying there. She cannot see this, so she uses her whole mind to dress herself, to sort her hair, to leave the bedroom then pause to sit on the staircase. Her plait seeps water between her neck and wallpaper. From downstairs, over the bannister, her mother laughs at something on the telly. The girl has this current moving in her arms and legs.

She climbs up inside herself for: a breath.

She snaps out of it when she hears the whispering of water. She kneels up and peers down into the hallway, where reflections are seeping down the floorboards and she sees a burble of flood coming from beneath the front door.

'Mum,' she calls. 'The hall's flooding.'

Stig shouts back. 'What's thudding?'

'No. Flooding. The hall's all wet.'

Her mother thunders through holding Declan. 'Fuck! She's right.'

Stig's bearded head sticks into the hall. 'Man alive.'

The girl holds onto Declan while her mother and Stig jam rolled up towels into the gap beneath the door, then they all go into the living room and the first thing you see is that the kitchen floor's a finger deep in water. It's trickling through the hole Stig made in the door.

He pushes past the girl, kicks off his trainers and stumbles down into it. His bare feet make fish sounds as he paces this way and that, looking for a solution. Her mother sits on the couch with Declan and the girl helps Stig find a tray to cover the broken window. She holds it in place while he uses brown tape except the wetness stops it from sticking. They've no other option but to block the hole with tea towels and carrier bags.

'There,' says Stig. 'Good as new.'

She sloshes across the kitchen and steps up into the living room. Still trembling, she sits down across from her mother. Everything from the neck down is made from worms, mixing themselves around. All the dimensions are wrong and the map's a mess – that feeling in dreams where you run and punch through sand. There's all these little pictures bubbling away in her mind, skirting around her insides, hiding when she tries to catch them face on.

'My jeans are wet,' she announces and she peels off her sodden trousers and hangs them over the back of the couch.

'What're you doing?' asks her mother.

'They got wet.'

Her mother has Declan standing up on her knees, letting him balance on his rubbery legs. 'Put some jammie bottoms on at least.'

She swallows, aware of the tongue in her head. 'I'm alright.'

Her mother sucks her mouth. 'Fine.'

Stig shouts through from the kitchen. 'Christ! These windows are leaking too.'

No one listens.

'Good boy,' her mother says to baby Declan. 'Look at them strong legs. Big strong legs.'

Baby Declan gurgles.

'You took ages to walk,' she tells the girl. 'And talk. And everything else really. Not like this wee man. We'll do things proper with this one. Yes we will. Yes we will.' She tickles his belly with her nose, her eyes clinging to the girl. 'No mistakes with *this* one.'

'Fuck it. It's a lost cause,' says Stig. He throws himself down beside the girl. 'We'll wait for the rain to go off and take it from there. I bet it'll mostly evaporate anyways. Water always evaporates in the end.' He stretches and then punches the girl in the side of the bare knee. 'Cheers for the help and so on.'

She can feel her mother's gaze upon her. There'll be times when she gets in from the school and she can feel her anger as soon as she opens the front door. A cloud of acid in the air, dread hanging in clumps along the hallway. Water dries on her legs and she crosses right over left and links right ankle behind left calf. Her mother watching is the heat of a sun.

'Are you actually sitting there like that?'

The girl nods to the telly.

'Really?'

'Aye.'

'Right,' snaps her mother. 'Braw. You two sit there then, like that.'

She hands Declan to Stig and Stig, oblivious, stands baby Declan on the floor between his legs. They watch him bounce for a couple of minutes. He grabs hold of his father's fingers like they're a lifeline and when he smiles his whole face is a torch of light.

The girl hides her hand in her inner thigh and she starts to twist and pinch at the skin. What would folk say at her funeral? People would get up at the front and say all the sweet things they couldn't when she lived. Gran and Grandad holding each other for support. And the boys. Maybe her mother, looking down into the open grave, saying into her own chest: I'm sorry, I'm so sorry.

'I'm getting a drink,' says Mum and she tips herself from the couch and through to the kitchen. She bangs cupboards doors for a while then comes back with vodka and orange juice and ice cubes. Half the glass goes in one and a gentle burp escapes.

'That's the ticket,' she says.

'Easy on, Angie,' says Stig. 'Slow yourself down.'

'Ha!' says Mum. 'This coming from the bloke that got through an entire twenty-four of cider in one sitting that time?'

'That was a festival,' he says. 'Everyone was getting pissed.'

'Well then, how dare you cast stones at me?'

The conversation's still within the realms of a joke – they're sort of semi-smiling and Mum's voice lilts with a lightness of touch, but she's already taken down the other half of vodka, shrugging from its content. 'Oo-ya,' she says and puts down the glass.

'Are you alright?'

'Never better,' she nods, quick and sharp, 'never better.'

The girl sort of shuffles forwards and holds the jeans.

'And where are you going?' asks Mum.

'Upstairs.'

Mum shakes her head. 'What's the matter? Aren't you wanting to sit and have a party with us? What have you got going on that's so important?'

'Nothing,' says the girl, and she shuffles back.

'Good,' says Mum.

She pats around the couch for her lighter and then lights up, wincing at the first cloud of smoke.

'There you go,' she says.

'I'd better take him through if you're doing that now,' says Stig, pulling baby Declan up.

'You are a useless example,' says Mum.

'Eh?'

'Look at this,' she laughs, pointing behind to the flooded kitchen. 'You're a useless example, mate. What sort of bloke is it can't even keep the water out?'

'Alright,' he says, sort of laughing and taking his baby through to sit on the stairs while Mum's smoking.

While he's gone, they don't even talk. When he returns, Mum scoffs, and so they sit together in quiet tenseness for a while, hours, watching the telly, Mum sometimes laughing bitterly, sometimes lighting up and half-finishing a fag, stubbing it out with a misplaced energy. She has several more vodka and juices and Stig has nothing, not even cans. You can feel his nerves at the swift mood that's taken hold of Mum, always glancing her way and sitting up straight like a naughty child.

'Here,' he says, later. 'I was just thinking. What if we went on a drive tomorrow, first thing?'

'Oh aye?'

'Aye. We could go on a drive and stop off for a pub lunch perhaps?'

'Hm,' says Mum. 'Maybe. And are you wanting me to come along too?'

'Eh? Course.'

'Not just you and Chloe?'

'No, don't be daft. I was meaning all of us going together. The four of us, I meant.'

'Oh. I see.'

'Why are you asking it like that?'

She doesn't answer at first. Instead, she finishes the current glass, tipping it back so the pale orange expands quickly and disappears down the gullet, down the neck, and she puts it on the floor and leans forward and her muscles ball out and the little dolphin leaps across her arm. You have never seen a woman like that. You have never seen a better woman.

'Stig,' she says. 'Let me ask you an honest question – see before, were you checking out my bairn's legs? Were you looking at my bairn?'

'Was I loo—?'

'It's an easy question. Were you looking at my bairn's legs? Were you leering at her?'

Stig considers them both and he's sort of squinting. He snorts a little bit.

'Where's this ...' he casts around for proper wording. 'Why did you ask me that just now?'

Mum does this bitter laugh. She coughs. 'Is this you avoiding the question?'

And the girl is floating herself harder than ever before, cutting away any veins that tie her brain to the shell of her skull, and her little collection of thoughts and voice is drawing around it cushion and cotton and moving roofward and is trying its tiny best to not be present – not to be seen. But some things are too hard to ignore, some

193

things barge into your earholes so you have to hear her say:

'Have you touched her as well, Stig?'

And Stig brings his son up to his chest and the girl herself speaks, saying, 'Mum! No!'

And Mum closes her eyes like the holy monks you see praying in the city sometimes – praying in orangey robes. She closes them and says, 'It was just a question. It was only a simple question.'

'Angie,' says Stig. 'Angie. Why—?'

'Have you touched her? Is that how come you took us off to this countryside?'

Very briefly he glances to the girl and he gives her this look, as if it's her that's generating the badness, as if she's whispered a bad report to her mother, and he says, 'No, course not.'

And it is just so...

It is sort of like when Guy Fawkes is happening somewhere and you haven't been taken to a show and from the bedroom window you can listen to unseen fireworks. It is the sadness of those explosions, of imagining others who are seeing them. Stig's face crumples; he does not understand. He hitches up the baby and opens his mouth, then closes it again.

Float. *Float*. Count.

'I think maybe you should get to your bed,' he says.

'I'm her mum, I say when she goes to bed.'

'I just think—'

'You've been acting like a perve since we got here,' Mum says. 'All the flirting, all the palling about. The pairs of yous hanging about on the hill like boyfriend and girlfriend.'

'Like boyfriend and girlfriend?' says Stig. 'Angie.

194

Angie. I can see that you aren't well. I can see that now, and I'm sorry if I took advantage. But to say this ... This is evil what you're saying to me.'

Mum's face barely moves now because of her sureness she's right. She's gone stiff in the features and is cocking her head to Stig's words, as if she's making them up herself and his talking is a part of her knowledge.

She looks to the girl. 'Go upstairs now, please.'

All these shouting voices rise through the floorboards – Mum screaming at Stig, Stig growling back, baby Declan screeching over the top of them both. The girl draws her knees to her chin as she perches on the bed. She rocks a bit. She tries to float but the anger's too urgent – it's coming up like heat. You can hear them moving around in furious pacing as they throw words at each other, as they connect and reconnect in their argument. This is an old habit for her. She's blocked out arguments through walls for as long as she can remember. For example: that man kicking at the door as she watched the electric fire and her mother held her ears.

That was her father. She knew it was, even then. She remembers him, of course.

One.

But she never thinks about him. Hardly anyone at school has a dad at home anyway.

Two.

That night. Her mother pulling her to the floor and the banging on the front door. The unbearable force of those kicks.

Three.

In a car. Thick-knuckled hand changing gears, fag butts spilling from the tiny ashtray and a string of beads chinking on the windscreen when the car turns. He asks her what she fancies doing, says they can go wherever she likes. She suggests swimming.

Four.

A car goes past. They're walking down a busy road together. She's tiny, compared to now, compared to the heavy male feeling at her side. He lifts her up onto his shoulders so she's bigger than anyone else around.

Five.

Fairy lights in green and red blink on then off again. The telly's showing a war film and all her Christmas present paper is balled up in a bin bag near the tree. No snow, but sleet. On the war film, this soldier's climbing through African waters and there's a knife and he's smiling from something and bombs explode from the earth. Another soldier falls onto a plunger and the bridge collapses like matches and the train plops down into the African waters.

'That's maybe what I told you,' her mother's saying in a tiny voice through on the house phone. 'But listen, Pete. Plans change. It's too confusing for her, you being here and then not. Come round in the New Year, maybe.'

A soldier says, '*Madness*,' and her mother walks in.

'I'm so sorry, pal. He isn't coming. I don't know what to say.'

She nods. She's heard both things her mother's said and believes them both because she has to.

On telly, a train falls into the waters.

The girl opens her eyes. Opens her eyes to hear the front door slamming, to hear the crunching of feet out in the drive. She creeps downstairs to check and Mum's standing at the head of the hallway. 'He's away.'

For a minute it looks as though things will go south,

196

because she glowers at the closed door for a couple of beats and you see a grey wing pass her eyes, but instead she unhunches her shoulders and untwists her mouth and says, 'Right. Let's get tea sorted.'

'Has he taken the car?' the girl asks.

'No, he's not taken the car. He's going down the road to get a signal. He's getting a lift off his mate.'

'Well, wha—'

'I said let's get tea sorted, didn't I? I said let's have a nice time.'

Mum rolls up the hems of her jeans and goes down into the kitchen, the girl following. The rainwater is warm. Before she starts making food, Mum pours another drink and it's half-and-half vodka to juice, so that the colour is like the weakest squash.

'Just like the old days,' she says. 'Just the two of us, a gang together.'

She boils them a pot of pasta twirls and the sauce comes pre-made in a fridge tub. The cooked pasta is enough to warm the sauce and there's also a garlic baguette but they forget to bake it. They sit up at the kitchen table, keeping their feet raised on the bars of their chairs.

'Do you like it?'

'Yeah,' says the girl, moving her twirls around inside the bowl.

'Just like at home.'

'Yeah.'

But there's sort of another person there with them. A darkness is across the table, a shadowy bulk which is everything that came before. It watches them chat and eat and it's laughing at the falseness of them.

'Mum,' the girl says. 'Stig. He never—'

'I don't want to hear it.'

'But honestly, he never. I don't know how come you said that but it didn't—'

'Will you shut up?'

'I—'

'Will you shut up, will you shut up, will you shut up? I'm losing my fucken *mind* here with you.'

'Alright.'

'You need to stop looking at me like that or else I'm going to lose my temper right now. Honestly, you do not understand the pressure I'm under. You do not.'

'I told you alright.'

Mum takes the two bowls and sloshes over to the sink to pile them up there and she holds onto the edge of it and is breathing, breathing, breathing.

'Oh Christ,' she whispers. 'Did I really ask him that? What did I say to him?'

'Mum, are we going away?'

'Just give me a minute. Give me a minute to think.'

The girl watches her mother's back rise and fall, stooped over the sink. She's whispering to herself now and because of the strangeness the girl has no choice but to see her grandparents again – the pair of them waltzing in just the lamps, their old hands clasping, notched into one another's shape.

Mum turns and she's back to her old self again, the doubt just a slip. 'No,' she says. 'No. We're staying here. We're here now and that's that. What time is it? It must be nearly time for your bed.'

She crosses the floor and brings the girl up by her shoulder, leading her out into the living room, into the hall, and the stairs and that area is unlit. For a brief moment in the darkness they have never been closer, the girl losing her edges and feeling they are these two souls that are one person, each eye of the same head looking out and seeing themselves different in the mirror.

In dirt, in black. Crumbs of earth are pushing against her mouth and she can barely open her eyes against the pressure of soil. Panic makes her flail and swim out of it. Upwards, upwards. She breaks out of the dirt and she's on the hillside and all this weather is pushing against her. Pushing her towards the white house below. She runs, the air catching her legs so she feels she's flying, and in through the back door and the kitchen's still flooded. Leaves and feathers blow about her head and the wind takes her voice away and all the time it's getting stronger, all the time, and it pushes her down onto the floorboards and the wind's pushing and rocking her and then she's in bed, awake. Her mother's standing over her. She's wet from sweat, on her face, in her hair – something's broken her. 'Let's go,' she says.

They go down the stairs. Her mother opens the front door and the girl takes their jackets from the peg. They pull their hoods up together as they walk across the front of the house. Her mother fumbles the keys and drops them as she tries to get the car unlocked. They're shivering and then they're locked inside. Around the car is a dome of night and rain drums on the roof like fingers and mother's and daughter's breaths are heavy and ragged.

'Where are we going?'

'Home,' says her mother. 'I don't know what's wrong with me. We're going home.'

The engine starts and the girl puts her seatbelt on. It's like that very first morning, thumbing the buckle in and watching her mother scurry up the garden path to the sound of Grandad's lungs. Her mother flicks on the headlights and they catch hold of something out in the dark – some small animal life that scurries off as soon as it's seen. The car stutters down the dirt path and when she looks back the house is red in the car's lamps.

Mum brings the car onto the road and the girl can feel all these strands coming loose as they drive; she's falling free, drifting through open, endless air.

IT TAKES A COUPLE OF HOURS TO REACH A TOWN. They pull up into a supermarket car park and her mother puts her seat right back to sleep, turns and draws up her legs. Above the supermarket the sky is lightening, night's deepness fading off into baby blue.

Baby blue.

Little Baby Declan McDonald, turning over in his sleep. Opening big eyes to look for comfort and his father's there but both are stranded in the middle of nowhere. They've fallen over in the dark, in a ditch at the side of the road, the little baby's wriggling body grasping and wanting for his father. Stig carries him up to the road but no cars are passing, no cars are coming from any direction. No cars.

She sits and watches the parking spaces fill up and she watches the workers in their uniforms walk round the back. At eight the shutters go up and the shop's open, so she can get them sandwiches and they take them down to the river behind the car park. People on bikes cycle past

201

on their way to work and her mother throws the tomatoes from her sandwich into the water. She looks like she's got the cold – eyes all puffy and her cheeks sagging. She throws her crusts into the river also and the ducks go crazy.

'What are we going to do?' she says.

The girl opens her crisps. She's not going to talk about it because talking it about it will lead to a discussion and any time spent discussing it could be time spent driving. She watches the ducks and finishes her crisps and puts the packet in the bin beside her. Across the river overgrown willows and reeds hang over and the current pulls their strands.

'Let's go,' she says and they walk back through the car park.

Her mother keeps wanting to stop, saying she's struggling to get her breath but the girl puts a hand on her back to keep them going. They hobble along together, weaving through the empty parking spaces.

They do up their seatbelts and drive on.

They come out of town and stop at a junction. One sign has their home's name, another her grandparents', and a flush of excitement rushes up inside the girl because she didn't even think she had the chance. She thought it was all lost.

'We need to go to Gran and Grandad's,' she says.

Her mother grips the steering wheel.

'We need to go and see them, Mum. You aren't well. They can look after us for a day or two before we go home.'

'I don't—'

'My mate might be out of the hospital by now,' she says. 'I might have to see him.'

Ally hadn't appeared until he became useful as an excuse. She nearly forgot he was in the hospital even, forgot about the beach and him swimming and nearly drowning. There was something wrong with her that she could do that. Forget an entire person like that. The car behind honks. You can see this man losing it in the rear-view mirror as Mum rubs her eyes. 'I just—' she says.

'Come on,' the girl says. 'It'll be fine.'

Her mother moans and flicks the indicator to the left.

Next town over, she gets shaky again, so they stop in a swimming pool car park and she sleeps in the back seat with this crusty old blanket. You can tell it's still the holidays because the place is full of people a bit older than the girl. They must be at the high school, looking at them. They go about in these packs together and the girls are already so pretty – they've got shapes the girl hasn't got yet and they cross their arms when they're laughing. She slides down the passenger seat when they pass the car and she can't believe she'll ever get there, ever be like them. She watches the older kids passing the car and gets such a knife of guilt about Ally and the boys that she closes her eyes to scare it off. Then another one comes, this time from Karen, for her rudeness the night Ally went into the water, then Mr Bell too. A knife for everyone she wronged.

Once Mum's awake, they come out of town and onto a wee road with fields all about. In another time it would be beautiful, but in this time her mother's barely keeping herself together. She leans all the way forward in her seat, biting at her lip and watching the road. They keep making wrong turns and getting lost.

'I think this is it,' her mother'll say and they'll drive

into a village but there won't be any other signs and they'll have to turn and go back onto the main road.

Her mother itches at her arms.

'Stop it,' hisses the girl. 'Stop scratching.'

'Can't help it, it feels like something's coming through. Tell me when I'm doing it.'

'You're doing it now.'

'I meant if I'm doing it again.'

'Mum, it's bleeding.'

So they pull over and her mother throws off the seatbelt and rakes long lines over her skinny arms. She's drawing red roads onto the skin.

'Stop it,' says the girl, but it doesn't help. 'I'm going to stand.' She goes to open her door but before she can, her mother's holding her by the wrist so tight.

'Stay here,' she says. 'Stay with me.'

The girl struggles. 'Let go.'

'I'm your mum and I'm telling you to stay here.'

Her mother's looking at her right up close in the face. She's got this feeling on her, like she's just figured something out about the girl. She lets go of the wrist.

'Listen: here's how it'll be,' she says. 'We'll find a place to stay tonight and in the morning we'll drive home. Everything's going back to how it was. We'll be happy and we'll forget this ever happened. Everything, we'll forget. It'll be the two of us and we'll be happy cause of that. We'll do a big clean and we'll get the bills sorted and we'll do all our dinners from scratch and you'll go to the big school in August. That's how it'll be. Alright?'

Quiet. 'Alright.'

Most of the B&Bs and guesthouses are booked up and they even try in the ones with *NO VACANCY* signs in the

204

windows. By the time they find one they've been round the village twice and they've come right to the outskirts so that her feet are killing her. The owner says she only has a single room going but that she can put out a camp bed for the girl. There's all these crosses on the walls with Jesus Christ himself crying upon them.

It's still light when they start to get hungry. A warm, clean summer evening. As they walk along the roads lined with stone bungalows the air is sweet with the smell of flowers baked in the heat of day. Her mother hobbles along beside her with her hood up and they're holding hands and their steps are in sync. A few streets over they find a corner shop and get some food to take back. The woman on the till eyes her mother and looks like she's going to say something, but the girl's saying, 'Thanks', and picking up the carrier bags before she can.

Up in the room they close the curtains and use the kettle for noodles.

The bathroom's cramped. The girl sits on the side of the bath as it fills, watching her face in the mirror as it disappears in condensation and listens to her mother sob through the door. Hot water turns cold before the bath's full so she has to make do. She can't get her whole head beneath the surface, so she rinses the shampoo out one side at a time. There's no soap so she uses shampoo for her face and armpits too.

As she brings her head out of the grey water for the last time, she notices that her mother's stopped crying and is talking.

'Just do it,' she's saying, then, 'No. Aye you can. Just do it.'

She's talking to herself in this high, sing-songish voice.

The girl lets the water out and dries herself with a tiny rough towel, then she puts the dirty clothes back on.

'I'll do it another day,' her mother sings. 'Never mind, never mind.'

The girl hangs her towel up.

They lie on their beds and watch the wee telly in the corner of the room. It's showing football. Neither of them like football but it's hard to work out how to change channels. Afterwards is the News and it doesn't make any sense at all, the stuff they're talking about. She remembers once her mother turning the news off at home in anger. 'Fucken news,' she said. 'Doesn't mean anything to folk like us, unless we're on it.' The girl feels almost nostalgic for that angry mother as she sneaks glances across the room at this one, on her side with hands flat between thighs. How she is now – this was the same as just before the girl went to her grandparents'. Lying down all the time, seeming flu-ish without symptoms. The girl learned how to make sauce for pasta and they had that twice a day. She already knew how to do the washing machine. They were getting by OK and then one morning, there she was, sitting on the couch while a car's engine turned over out in the street.

'What'll we do then?' she asks across the bedroom.

'Go home,' her mother grunts. 'I already told you.'

'I just think,' says the girl, 'maybe we should go to Gran and Grandad's, at least for a bit. Does that not make sense?'

This rouses her mother, just enough to rise up in the bed. 'I need you to do me a favour,' she says.

'What?' says the girl.

'Tell me what Stig did.'

The girl clenches. She gets that soreness in her legs so that they must be held taut.

'Fucken men,' her mother says, misunderstanding. 'These fucken ... men.' She spits the word out like a seed. 'Listen: all I ever wanted – all I ever asked for – was to be quiet, for it to be quiet. Deep down like. Did you know that? All the pubs and that, that wasn't proper. I just wanted to sit down in a room and be warm and still ... And, like, there's this someone in the next room and he's a man but he's in the next room and he's in there and it doesn't make me feel bad that he's not beside me and also I'm not glad he's not anywhere near me. I just feel good cause I'm in a quiet room and this man's in the next room and he's sort of mine.'

She's not even talking to the girl. It's not clear she even knows the girl's there.

'But they won't ever fucken let you have it. None of them. Not your boyfriend, not your mate, not even your family. None of them'll let you be quiet. All they want is for your brain or your head or whatever it is to be empty and nothing and they all want to go marching in, shouting, moving stuff about, fingers everywhere. Why's it so hard to be quiet? What's wrong with peace? When that's all you've ever wanted your whole entire life?'

She scrambles up, rakes at her arms and her pupils have gone still again, lasering the girl.

'You want to know something? You're selfish. And greedy. You think it's all yours,' she points a finger at the girl's forehead, 'what goes on up there. But it's not. It's mine too. It's everyone's. You think you can just say nothing and that's enough. It isn't. Don't you care about what I'm saying? Don't you give a shite? Well show it if you do. Be angry. Let them see you're angry.'

The girl's getting this animal – this animal rushing up, flying into her mouth from below.

'What happened with Stig,' her mother says, 'that happened with Uncle Bobby too, with me, only it happened worse. It happened when I was just this bairn and we used to drive down the caravan at weekends and holidays and Mum and Dad would go to the dancing and him and Pat'd look after me. Jesus. I was only this bairn, only sixteen maybe, and he—'

She snorts up a wad of grief.

'I never said – I never said to no one. I told my mum and dad but then they spoke to him and they asked me if I meant it and I said, No. I said I was making it up, because I couldn't bear it. I couldn't bear for them to know that side of me. That dirt. And then I was away that summer, after I'd met Pete and he gave me you.'

She coughs, hiccups, blinks.

'When folk asked how come I moved away when I had you, how come I never ever went home, I told them your grandad used to beat me up, cause even then I couldn't let them see my dirt. I never told the truth again – not once. I made this hardness around me, this sort of sharpness—'

She turns to the ceiling, all distorted from remembering.

'And now Stig too. I always thought he was good. These fucken men, doing whatever they feel like, and we're meant to sit and take it? And we're meant to sit and act like none of it's happened? Now it's just us.'

The girl can't listen to what's being said. All she has the power to do is say, 'It's not just us.'

I have a family. I've got pals. I have a future that's coming towards me fast. I have me just now, and me before, and me a week from now. They're all mine – every last one of them – and she can't even believe how bad that tastes, those words that she spoke. She can't believe these thoughts are coming now and flocking around her mother and causing the last of the light to be dulled in her eyes.

Her mother lands feet on the floor and sighs. She says, 'Was it really that bad?'

'Was what?' says the girl.

'Our life.'

That night by the water and the men coming home; a hundred other nights the same; her mother's theft, removing tags from her top, striding down the high street; leaving the girl alone, at night.

'Sometimes it was bad,' says the girl.

'Believe me,' her mother says. 'I never knew. I thought we were having fun. I thought it was that we were a gang together.'

'You were a gang yourself,' says the girl.

Her mother hunches over further, nearly kissing her knees. 'Remember that time though when you were little and we did the boats down the park?'

The girl doesn't remember.

'Course you do,' says her mother. 'Think about it. It must've been the holidays from the school and remember we got the bus down from beside the flats and we got a junior ticket each? You were laughing so hard at your old mum getting herself on with a bairns' ticket! We got the bus down the park and you didn't want to go to the swings bit because you probably never wanted to look like a baby being there with your mum, so we went to the boats bit? And remember the old boy was there and said the boats were so-much a shot and I gave him this kiss on the cheek so that he'd let us on for half?'

The girl's getting this picture of boats on water – of her feet hidden in their boat's body. Her mother powering on the oars.

'See?' says her mother. 'You do so remember. We did the boats for ages, didn't we? We went right around twice or three times and then we sat about just floating and I remember you said it was very pretty. And! Oh, and! Remember we went onto the island? The island in the middle? We took the boat into the trees and you could sort of drag it up onto the dirt and there was all these geese or ducks or whatever there? I know you remember that. Because listen: didn't we go right across the island to the other side and we were waving to the folk in the park on the other side, from where you couldn't see there was boats, and shouting that we were stuck, didn't we? And then when we got back around the boat had slipped off into the water and I had to go out into the water to reach it and I lifted you in so that you wouldn't get wet and we took the boat back and the old boy was going loopy because of the time we were?'

'I do remember,' says the girl.

'There,' says her mother.

'It's not enough.'

Her mother leans back. She swallows and says, 'There's a thing about you I never put there.'

'What do you mean?'

Her mother rubs at her eyes' corners. 'You've got this streak of something I've never known. I don't know where it came from but I'm glad you've got it.'

And then there's quietness in the room, the two of them on their beds, watching the walls and the girl thinking, How can this ever end?

'Maybe it came,' says the girl, 'from Dad.'

'Maybe,' nods Mum.

'What was he like?'

Mum tips back a little. 'Just this bloke. I don't know, he was my mate. He was alright, he was nuts.'

The girl holds her own hand. 'You really can't remember?'

'Nope.'

And she's not even lying – she doesn't know – and she's hiccupping up all her sadness. 'What'll happen with us?' her mother asks and because there's nothing left the girl gets up from the camp bed and goes to her and helps her lie back.

'I don't know,' says the girl.

'Will we be fine, Chloe?' asks her mother.

The girl brushes stray hairs from the tackiness of her mother's brow and there's this song from childhood she hums. Her mother smiles because of it, letting lines on her face go smooth. The girl hums this song and brushes her mother's brow and there's just so much —

In another room a clock chimes, so she sits. The earliest morning is showing behind curtains and the room stinks of their bodies and the mountain range of her mother sleeps quiet over on the bed. The girl sits up in her camp bed. She has dreamed of nothing.

She unballs her clothes from beneath the bed and dresses herself silently. She packs her bag and takes a twenty-pound note from her mother's purse. She closes the door as she leaves and it makes no more sound than a kiss. Past the cars on the road and her mouth is gummy and thick and she knows something important's been cut away from her. A chunk of herself's been trimmed.

Aye, this is true. But she's still walking, isn't she? She's still crossing the road. She's still looking at signs and keeping her head down and never once looking back.

THE TRAIN PLUNGES ACROSS THE SKIN OF the land like a knife. A crowd gets on at Falkirk High and the conductor tells her she'll have to change trains in the city. There's all these people and adverts and suitcases in the big main station that she has to dodge around. When she's on the platform, she closes her own eyes for a moment because they hurt, and when she opens them again her train's leaving. She walks along her platform to the open air and finds a bench. Clouds race through the sky and she can smell the perfume of train fuel.

Birthday morning. Her second last one – ten years old. Waking up sick with excitement. The couch through the living room full of presents. And Mum coming in, smiling and hugging her and wishing her a happy birthday. They sit on the floor and open gifts. There's a diary that she's going to write in every single day. There's a tool that helps you make your own bracelets. There's a book that shows you all the kings and queens that the country's ever had.

212

While they have breakfast her mother puts a film on and tells her she doesn't need to go to school if she doesn't want to. They can do whatever she wants. They do makeovers on each other and have some birthday cake even though it's morning still.

Looking up into the sun makes her sneeze. She sees the next train's coming in because it has the town written on the front. It won't be long now. She needs to keep herself together for a little while longer. The train's coming in and the last batch is getting off and she's moving through them to reach the doors and climb inside.

Here's later on the birthday. She's got the window seat on the bus and the city's so full she has to count to calm herself down.

You can throw brown coins into a fountain in the museum's foyer and the whole roof in the next room is filled with a whale. You don't even notice it until you're in there for a minute and you look up to see the ceiling and instead there's a whale there. Its mouth is furry and brown and the sign says that it's for filtering because when the whale was alive it could only eat tiny sea creatures. There was also a whole bank of glass cases. Some had moths and butterflies but this one, right in the darkest corner, was full of tiny birds. They were spaced out with pure whiteness between them, exotic with wings like jewels and with long beaks, or stout beaks and narrow wings like knives.

In another room there were metal balls called something-generators. These smooth metal balls like what sinks are made from and you went up to them and your fingers kind of itched as you held them to the curve. You and Mum put a hand on each one and felt it working on you and there was a mirror so you could see the electricity was making your hair levitate! It was like you both were floating or swimming and your hairs were moving around and you could see you both had the same colour.

Before you leave you go back to see the animals one last time – your favourite bit. You missed this one display which was in a corner and was sort of dark. It was a crocodile in a swamp, half-crawling into the fake water from the grassy bank and smiling and watching the girl. Some facts about crocodiles were: they had *the strongest bite of any predator*, could live to over *seventy years old*, shed their *scales* one-by-one, and that nearly *every baby died* within its first month.

And then you notice that from the crocodile's smiling mouth is this baby crocodile peeking from between the fangs – meaning this is a mum and its child. The baby is nestled on the big pink tongue and its skinny tail trails from the mum's teeth like a string of pasta, and for a moment you think, Oh no! The mum's going to eat the baby! But the sign goes on to say that the mum crocodile will carry its babies round in its mouth like this for protection, after they've hatched.

The baby looks so safe in there, peering and grinning from its cradle of fangs.

The second train deposits her at the end of the line and she walks from there to her grandparents'. Before she goes in, she stops with her hand on the rail. The paint is cracked and peeling and shows the steel beneath. It's cold in her hand. The street's empty and no cars go past and all the windows in all the houses glow.

Nothing moves. Nothing moves, until up in the sky a

214

sheet of starlings moves past, the rapid motion of their wings and callings unobserved in the clear night. Once they vanish, nothing moves.

She turns and pulls herself up the steps and the bead curtain rattles as she opens and closes the door behind herself. All of the air solidifies when she walks into the kitchen. Grandad looks into someplace and his hand tries to find a thing to hold, except it's missing.

The following night a call comes through. She wakes to the phone's chirruping from the hallway, then this stumbling footfall – Grandad walking out of sleep. You hear him go, 'Hello?' and the girl knows what's coming.

It's going to be her mother, saying she needs to get home. Perhaps she'll arrange for Gran and Grandad to drive her back, probably that same day. And what can they do? They can't say no. They can't keep her here if that's not what her mother wants. The girl pushes herself further down the sheets and her fingers hold onto the mattress.

Grandad goes, 'You're joking.'

There'll be black moods that pollute every corner of their flat, there'll be these silences that turn the girl inside out with fear. What if Stig's back? What if baby Declan's back? She can't look them in the eye ever again, can she?

There's a crashing in the hall and then Gran's coming through too and joining the commotion.

The girl's doing her floating trick.

'Who is it?' says Gran. 'What's she saying?'

'She's not saying anything,' says Grandad and their voices recede.

You can just see how it'll go. It's so obvious. In a moment, once it gets too much, she's going to creep

215

through and they'll tell her the news – she's off, she's leaving, this is it. And she's not even seen the boys yet; she doesn't know if Ally's alive or dead. Those few nights, away with her mother, she kept them down low in a hidden compartment. You couldn't see things like that with her mother in the room – there was no space left over.

She pushes the duvet off and goes across the floor. The room says nothing and there's no movement from Karen above. She treated Karen so badly – treated Mr Bell so badly too – and now there'll be no chance to make amends. Up against the door, she listens. The gloss paint cools her ear's cartilage but nothing can be heard. She's listened through so many doors in her time that it's second nature to push against it and move around and find the pathways sound can make.

Nothing, so she inches it open. They're talking in the living room, but only in whispers. Off she goes, trailing her knuckles along the wall, until she's just outside.

'I just can't believe she would do something so stupid,' Gran's saying.

Grandad doesn't reply.

'Alec,' she says. 'You have to say something.'

The girl shows herself and both faces jerk up from their hands – they're holding hands – to catch her. Both of them are white, both of them are doubled over from something.

Gran says, 'Pet!'

You can see Grandad's sort of coasting. He's sort of floating himself too.

The girl says, 'Was it Mum?'

'No,' says Gran.

'She's away,' Grandad says. 'She's gone away!'

216

And he's nearly smiling from pain. And he's baring his teeth and rocking and his pain's coming through with such might that the house itself starts to quicken. You can feel bricks move between bricks. You hear floorboards moan.

'Away?' says the girl.

'Away,' laughs Grandad.

'It was the police on the phone,' says Gran. 'They found her. We have to—' But she can't go on. She's holding her husband's hand and the house is stretching them from the girl.

'What happened?' she says.

'Nothing,' says Gran.

'She was in this building,' says Grandad. 'In this building, off the road. They don't know how yet and she's away, she's—'

A figure emerges from the gluey mist, this figure moving slow across grasses so that the cows have to low and snort and move aside. She's dragging her trainers and lurching and you can see in her eyes that she's without sleep or rest or nourishment. She moves aside these tall reeds in the depth of a valley so that she can pass and like before there's standing water there too. She trudges through regardless and again the water seeps into the fabric of her trainers and chills the bones and skin of those clawlike appendages, increasing her hobbling. Only one word is on her mind – she herself is only one word. The skin of her arms is coming away in pieces. Her true self is pushing through these rags to cast off the scales she crafted, but this emergence does not hasten her journey. It drags on her, makes the climb from the valley endless. The cows return to their places and she is forgotten by

217

them as she trudges beyond sight. She's crawling now as nothing remains to hold her upright. She claws fistfuls of shining pasture for ballast, pulls herself along a ridge to the moor's ending and from a tussle of bracken and coiled fencing-wire sprout a tree and a kissing gate. She herself is only one word and she passes the gate and leans for a moment against the wood. Cars are passing down on the road, again and again and again. There is no lonelier sound than these engines' hum in the still morning. She coughs and brings up a grape of something to her palate. Downwards is easiest so she goes this way, wincing at each footfall on the slope. A segment of road peeks from the moor's furthest curve and she follows it, helping herself to emerge with these quick bursts of scratching to the forearms, the neck, the lower back. Only her face remains unscraped but it's so hard and delicate that it doesn't need much to explode. This squarish greenness appears by the pathway she finds. She totters towards the greenness and it reveals itself – a static caravan, built on black boards and with farming paraphernalia stacked around its perimeter.

So this is it, a caravan. She could nearly laugh.

She tries the door and it lets out a stink of mould. She sort of falls inside. It isn't derelict because there are clean mugs lined up on the counter and newspapers by the chair and the black blooms of decay on the roof and walls have been scrubbed away here and there. There's a kitchen area and a low couch and in the corner a closed door. You can smell a man and there is no softness anywhere.

A caravan. She could nearly laugh.

She tries to sit down in the chair and she manages it for a time. The windows are obscured by netting and she can't get the cold out. She let it in but it won't get out and now she's sheltered these great racking shivers are cramping up her spine, her shoulders. But it's only herself trying to get out. It's only herself pushing at the breakages of her scales to be revealed; the skin's taken the brunt of it and now she can live. She pries off the sodden trainers and socks and tries to operate the flesh down there. She kind of gasps, then goes onto the carpet and once as a girl she was on the floor of a caravan too. She needs some heat inside – this is the issue. Needs to get some heat inside to warm this cold blood. Once the heat's back her feet will follow; she'll be allowed to shed the last of this skin.

She mouths a word.

The low couch has a bundle of used black tarp that she shuffles towards. She pulls this down onto the floor and wraps it around herself and chases the sleep that's skirting the outskirts of her mind. It proves to be uncatchable; she's in this state of semi-waking that clings to her and will not be washed. And her inner self, waiting to tear open the old, is busy with energy and plus her feet are coming alive with insects. She throws off the tarp and sees, over on the counter: the caravan's hob. A little crown of blackened metal and the dials beside it – a red canister below. She crawls and reaches up to thumb the dial so that hissing begins. The heat will enter soon enough. She rolls back and lets the hardness of the floor flatten her backbone and holds the feet just above the ground. She blinks and waits. She is one word. This moment will be endured, as will the next on its heel. She takes off her jeans and her legs breathe in the mould, remembering the feel of caravan carpet. They remember that hot itching of nipping carpet thatch, that slow burn of their movement against it. Even in this place she can hear the cars passing again and again, so she rolls onto her side to peer up at the counter, to check the heat. It's hissing alright but nothing's reaching her. This will be endured and there is no lonelier sound and she is one word.

Look! There are these birds cascading behind the netting. She wipes hair from her forehead like her own daughter did, in that bed. Her own daughter wiped away her hair and hummed a song she had passed on in infancy. It was called 'Son of a Preacher Man' and she's producing it herself now – this tremulous hum that is the throat's movement just before giggling. Her yellow eyes close and she can see the daughter again, standing over, her narrow fingers wiping her face. In the caravan she's smiling and they're both humming the song she passed on. There were other things she passed on too but they were only a fraction of what she contained. What a shame. There were some things, so many things, that she missed. But how could you say them? There were some things that there was no language for. Some things she wanted to pass on that she was yet to know.

She herself is now only one word and one word is rising within her, coming up past her tonsils to form a bubble that exists translucent for one … two … three …

Or maybe it was nothing like that at all.

After all the madness, the girl slips into the bedroom. For a while she stands in one spot, swaying, because she can't stop seeing that bubble. What was inside? What was the word? She waits for it …

In an instant, she's on the bed, tearing up the sheets and ploughing her fingers into pillows. She's pushing her forehead into the woodchip and moving it so the texture grates her skin. There's nothing coming in from the outside and she needs there to be. She needs something and it isn't coming. It's just her, bound up in these sheets, jerking around and gurning and punching the mattress and none of that helps because she's still there and she can't get rid of this girl.

The room doesn't speak a word – there is nothing to see her.

CODA

In the hospital, people in dressing gowns are milling around on the lino, in wheelchairs or using walking sticks or wheeled trolleys, between the shop and the cafe. Gran buys fruit and sweets and they take the lift up to the ward. A pregnant woman goes past. She's being pushed in a wheelchair and her stomach's massive between her legs. The girl pauses at a corner to watch her go, to watch the vastness of her torso and the puce desperation of this woman's face.

They walk past her down the corridor, looking for the right room, and you can hear all different sorts of breathing from behind curtains. Someone shouts, twice, as they pass. And then they turn the corner and voices are skating along the floor, ringing on wall-charts.

'Darryl, you must be the king of clowns if you think I'm letting you borrow my PlayStation,' says Ally. 'Mind what happened when I lent you my cards?'

Ally's being swallowed up by the bed. His skin is as pale as the sheets, his arms and chest as bony as the bars of the frame. But none of that's stopping him. He's moving in place, touching the bars of his bed, cocking his head with annoyance.

'Well, well, well,' he says, clocking her and Gran. 'Here she is. Lady Muck herself. Won't even bother to come and see her old mate when he's laid up in the hospital. She's too important, lads.'

'Hiya, Ally,' she says.

'Hiya yourself,' he says.

Darryl and Chris stand up as they get behind the curtain and are sort of sheepish around Gran. Ally says the mums are along getting coffees from the machine, so Gran goes after them.

'Fuck, you should've seen it, Stretch,' he says. 'I had tubes in me everywhere they could fit tubes. Sorry to not be a gentleman about this but I even had this tube in my knob. How about that?'

'That's rank,' she says.

'You're telling me,' says Ally. 'I was the one had to waz out it.'

She's laughing and screwing up her face until Darryl pipes up. 'So where've you been then?'

It's the question she's been dreading all the way here in the car. She's been sweating this question because she's yet to answer it for herself.

'I was with my mum,' she says.

'Not bad for some,' says Ally. 'This your big businesses mum?'

'No,' she says. 'It wasn't like that.'

'But you're back?' says Chris.

'Aye,' she says. 'I didn't like it.'

The lads look at her for this one beat and that's it. Ally starts going on about the trials and hardships of the young man in the world of medical care. He tells of everyone who's watched him pee, the mashed potato he's suffered, the nurses yet to return his persistent affections. He tells them he wishes he could've held off on nearly drowning for a few weeks so at least he'd have missed school for it.

The girl makes the mistake of catching eyes with the man in the bed next to Ally.

'I fought in the war,' this neighbour announces.

'Aye, alright big man,' says Ally, then to them, *'He's always like that.'*

The man in the next bed waves his hand. 'I fought in the war, and for what? To be treated like a silly wee lad?'

He isn't old enough to have fought in the war. It looks like he's shaved his own head.

'What's so good about this chump,' he nods at Ally, 'that he's getting all these guests and I'm getting eff all? Them nurses is blocking my guests.'

'Give it a rest, would you?' says Ally. 'This is my one moment of pleasure a day.'

The neighbour leans in. 'I want to tell you all a secret.'

'Aw, hang this,' says Ally and he shambles himself out of the big bed and gets shiny new crutches down from the unit. 'Come on,' he says. 'I'll show you the telly room.'

The neighbour sits back in his bed and they get a couple of steps down the corridor before they let their laughter out from his performance and Ally's laughing so hard that this nurse rushes over to tell him off and that just makes it so much worse.

He leads them down the corridor to the telly room and Gran's standing with these other women who must be the boys' mums. All faces turn to them and this one woman, with the same red hair as Ally, holds him by the neck and asks how he's feeling. Her face is washed with such an expression of love that the girl has to turn away, knowing this is a look that is lost to her, unsure, in fact, if she has ever received it.

The couch screams as she flops down onto the plastic wrapping. On telly's a game of golf. She watches it for a bit until she feels like screaming too. She gets up to look for the remote, flipping over cushions and opening the cabinet. Not really looking for the remote though. She's building herself up ...

It's over on the wall, hanging, until it's in her hands. Three faces – two adults and one red squashed baby, brand new. That's her dad, the man there, and the other face ...

When she looked at this photo before, she knew she was the same as the baby, just as fresh and as terrified. But it's not like that anymore. Before she could sense that baby inside herself, twisting with fear, but no longer. Now she barely recognises the tiny features peeking from a knitted blanket.

In comes Gran, carrying the plates. She puts them down on the dining table. 'It's a good photo,' she says from behind the girl.

'What age am I there?'

'Oh, a few hours old. That was the first day we saw you. That was when Angie still stayed at home, with us.'

'Right.'

'It's a lovely photo.'

'I spoke to her about him,' she says, turning.

Gran's face is calm, not what the girl had expected. 'What do you think?'

The girl can't answer – doesn't know how.

'Give me a second.'

There's noises of drawers opening and closing from the bedroom – Gran's looking for something. In time, she comes back with a slip of paper which she presses into the girl's hand. It's an address.

'I never liked him, I have to say, but it's up to you,' Gran says, then, 'Come and get your tea.'

Here's how it goes. They get around that small table and have tea together and Gran's going on about what Barbara's been up to this time – she's speaking on the computer with a waiter from the Mediterranean and Gran's convinced it'll all end in tears. You can see these men swing golfs clubs in Grandad's glasses and he's saying, 'Aye,' and, 'I know,' to whatever Gran's asking.

'Oh,' says the girl. 'I don't have any stuff for next week.'

'No,' says Gran. 'Of course you've not. We'll go into town on Friday and get your uniform and pens and whatever else.'

'Is it that time already?' says Grandad.

'It is,' says Gran. 'The big school.'

'You don't call it *big* school,' scoffs the girl.

'Oh, I don't know,' smiles Gran. 'Sorry if I'm not cool enough for you.'

She helps with the washing, pushes her hands down into the hot basin and you can feel the metal of knives and forks swimming in the water. She's got all these days coming towards her. All these days, and there are girls up at the kitchen window, steaming the glass to look in, and they're the past and the future and they belong to her.

In the hospital, this pregnant woman goes past. She's being pushed in a wheelchair and her stomach's massive

229

between her legs. Her cheeks are wet and purple and her fringe is splayed across like a dark web. You can sense the baby inside her is desperate to get out. It can only be a moment away.

The girl must have been born here, she realises, in this hospital. All those years ago, the girl would have been wheeled along, encased in her mother's skin. She would have been brought out into the light, face all creased and smeared with insides. For a while they would have been together, the three of them – *Angie, Pete, Chloe*. She wonders who held her first, who wiped the matter from her eyes?

They've finished with Ally and she's leaving the lift with Gran – and now here's her mother, coming down the corridor with the baby girl in her arms. She squeezes past them to catch the lift, cradling the bundle of cloth. She squeezes past into the lift and Gran hurries the girl into the foyer. She falls back, watching as her mother stands in the lift, then looks around. The wing of her shoulder lowers and you can see the girl's face.

You have to, the girl says, watching.

The lift doors are closing and the dream is evaporating, but in the closing gap, her mother draws back the cloth and you can see the girl's own tiny face.

You have to.

She strokes the baby's face with one finger and the doors close and her mother's face is washed with such ...

You could see it!

You could see it perfect there and there was no language for how she held the girl.

It was there though – you could see it. How could it not be there if you could look through that closing gap and see it?

ACKNOWLEDGMENTS

Thank you to:

University of Edinburgh School of Literatures, Languages & Cultures.

My agent Cathryn and everyone at Sandstone Press.

Alan G, Allyson S, Dilys R, Rodge G.

Alice T, Amanda B, Candace A, Florence V, for sound advice / warm hospitality.

My family, who thankfully are not featured (much) in the preceding story.

www.sandstonepress.com

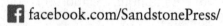 facebook.com/SandstonePress/

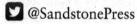 @SandstonePress